Drake spoke furiously. "You don't understand me at all, Nicole, or you wouldn't accuse me—"

"I wasn't accusing—"

"Or interrupt me—"

"You interrupt me, too," she reminded him.

"You never know when to stop, Nicole. You push and push until I'm ready—" He gripped her arms and pulled her against him. "Until I have to—"

Before Nicole had a chance to move or think or even breath, his mouth covered hers in a hard kiss. She reacted violently, struggling against him, but Drake was too strong for her. Every moment against his chest made her stunningly aware of her body pressed to his, of the heat he'd ignited inside her.

And then, suddenly, she stopped fighting. Instinctively she surrendered to her own raging desire burning through her. For the first time in her life, she felt the deeply feminine need to envelop, to absorb this man into her very being. Drake had taken her in his arms and turned her into a wild thing. . . .

WHAT ARE *LOVESWEPT* ROMANCES?

They are stories of true romance and touching emotion. We believe those two very important ingredients are constants in our highly sensual and very believable stories in the *LOVESWEPT* line. Our goal is to give you, the reader, stories of consistently high quality that may sometimes make you laugh, sometimes make you cry, but are always fresh and creative and contain many delightful surprises within their pages.

Most romance fans read an enormous number of books. Those they truly love, they keep. Others may be traded with friends and soon forgotten. We hope that each *LOVESWEPT* romance will be a treasure—a "keeper." We will always try to publish

LOVE STORIES YOU'LL NEVER FORGET
BY AUTHORS YOU'LL ALWAYS REMEMBER

The Editors

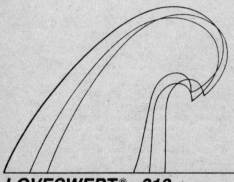

LOVESWEPT® • 313

Barbara Boswell
Ms. Fortune's Man

BANTAM BOOKS
TORONTO • NEW YORK • LONDON • SYDNEY • AUCKLAND

MS. FORTUNE'S MAN

A Bantam Book / March 1989

If you would be interested in receiving protective vinyl
covers for your Loveswept books, please write to this address
for information:

Loveswept
Bantam Books
P.O. Box 985
Hicksville, NY 11802

ISBN 0-553-21965-0

Published simultaneously in the United States and Canada

Bantam Books are published by Bantam Books, a division
of Bantam Doubleday Dell Publishing Group, Inc. Its trademark, consisting of the words "Bantam Books" and the
portrayal of a rooster, is Registered in U.S. Patent and
Trademark Office and in other countries. Marca Registrada.
Bantam Books, 666 Fifth Avenue, New York, New York 10103.

PRINTED IN THE UNITED STATES OF AMERICA

O   0 9 8 7 6 5 4 3 2 1

One

"Mr. Austin, there's a young woman here to see you. She *insists* on seeing you immediately."

The fact that Carmen, his secretary, had called him by his last name was Drake Austin's first clue that something wasn't quite right. Added to that was her presence here in his office. Normally, she would have used the intercom to inform him of a visitor's arrival. Since Carmen was positively gifted in sending uninvited callers on their way, but felt compelled to notify him personally about this one portended something unusual.

His curiosity aroused, Drake glanced up from the portfolio of photographs he was studying. "Did she say why she insists on seeing me, Carmen?"

The usually unflappable Carmen came as close as Drake had ever seen her come to losing her cool. "She has a baby with her, Drake. A baby boy. And she claims it's yours!"

Drake leaned back in his chair. "She does, hmm?" His mouth curved into a wry smile. "You have to give the lady credit for a novel approach, Carmen. She's certainly managed to get our attention."

"I'm convinced this is more than an attention-getting ploy, Drake," Carmen replied worriedly.

"I've been intercepting would-be models and aspiring photographers for you for the past five years, and I'll bet anything that this girl isn't either one. And the—"

She stopped in midsentence as the office door was flung open. A young woman in a flowered sundress and sandals stood in the doorway, holding a baby boy clad in a bright yellow sunsuit printed with ducks. Her long, dark brown hair, curling at the ends, hung shiny and thick, halfway down her back. The baby grabbed a fistful of it and tugged.

"It's no use plotting to get rid of me," Nicole Fortune announced, her dark blue eyes flashing. "I won't leave until I've talked to Drake Austin." The baby in her arms uttered a loud string of syllables, almost matching the fierceness of her tone. Nicole attempted to extricate her hair from his determined little fingers, but the baby refused to let go.

Carmen looked totally nonplussed. Drake Austin merely smiled.

He stood up. "It's okay, Carmen, I'll talk to her."

"Drake, are you sure?" Carmen looked uncertain, but when he smiled again reassuringly, she gave a brief nod and swiftly left the office, closing the door behind her.

Nicole watched her go, then turned to face Drake Austin. She gulped. He was so tall! At least six feet four, and as if his height weren't imposing enough, his frame was muscular and solid, doubling the impression of commanding strength. He was a handsome man, with deep-set pale blue eyes, a fine, straight nose, and a well-shaped mouth. His thick shock of dark hair was longish in the back, slightly overlapping the collar of his deep raspberry-colored polo shirt. His jeans were well-worn and faded, accentuating his trim waist and flat belly and the powerful strength of his thighs.

Nicole jerked her gaze away from him, unsettled by the tingles of awareness shooting through her. Hadn't she read in a magazine article tracking his career as one of the country's foremost critically acclaimed and financially successful photographers, that "Drake Austin exudes a virile, sexual intensity to which no woman is immune"? The description rattled around in her brain. It was true. She would have to be dead to remain unaware of the man's potent appeal.

But she couldn't let it affect her and her mission, Nicole silently lectured herself. It would hardly help baby Robbie if she were to turn into mush in his father's presence. She drew a long, bolstering breath and opened her mouth to speak.

Drake Austin beat her to it. "You have my complete attention, honey," he said, his voice deep and low and smooth. "Why don't you tell me what you've come to say?"

Nicole looked quickly at his face. He was watching her, his blue eyes, several shades lighter than her own, gleaming with something akin to . . . amusement?

"You think this is funny?" she blurted out.

Nicole was well aware that her greatest failing lay in being too impulsive and outspoken. Unfortunately, she was often too impulsive and outspoken to catch herself at it. Her carefully rehearsed speech never had a chance to be heard as the impetuous words tumbled out of her mouth.

"Well, my coming here is no joke, Drake Austin." She took a brave step toward him, tightening her arms around the baby. "This is your son."

Drake arched his eyebrows. "So you told Carmen," he said calmly. "Does the little guy have a name?"

Nicole's jaw dropped open and she gaped at him. She'd expected him to rage at her or to deny his paternity or to threaten her, perhaps to do all three. She was so taken aback by his nonchalant response that she murmured, "Robbie," while continuing to stare dazedly at him.

"Robbie." Drake crossed the office in a few relaxed, rangy strides. "I like it." He stood beside her and offered the baby his finger. Robbie's tiny fingers closed around it and he studied it curiously. "Short for Robert?"

Robbie carried Drake's finger to his mouth to gnaw. Nicole immediately pulled the baby away. Drake Austin was standing much too close. She took several steps back to put some distance between them. He was so big that she felt dwarfed, an unfamiliar and disconcerting feeling. At five feet seven, she was used to being the tall and imposing one. "His full name is Robert Richard," she said tersely, then added, "Austin. Robert Richard Austin."

Robbie grinned up at Drake, showing off his four pearly-white front teeth, two on top, two on the bottom. His eyes were large and wide-set, a rich chocolate brown in color, fringed by thick, dark lashes. He had a full head of baby-fine dark hair, several strands of which spiked straight out from the top of his head.

Drake grinned back at the baby. "How old is he?" he asked conversationally, "Miss—Mrs.—?"

"Ms.," Nicole snapped. "My name is Nicole Fortune. Robbie turned nine months yesterday."

"Ms. Fortune." Drake repeated dryly. Humor lit his light blue eyes. "I'll refrain from making one of the jokes you must get very tired of hearing."

She almost thanked him. She was heartily sick of those inevitable puns on her name. Nicole quickly caught herself. Thank him? She was here for Robbie's sake, not to fall victim to this—this slick libertine's charm!

"Robbie is nine months old," she repeated, her voice rising with emotion. "And you haven't contributed a cent toward his support. It's a father's duty to provide for his child, *Mr. Austin*. It's not only the law, it's—it's a moral imperative! Your behavior is unconscionable! You're a rich man, yet you're willing to shirk your responsibility to your baby and—"

"You're absolutely right, Ms. Fortune," Drake interrupted laconically. "It is a father's duty and a legal and moral imperative to provide for his child. I'll never argue with that. So . . ." He held out his arms. "Give little Robbie to me and I'll take him home and provide for him."

Nicole recoiled, as if he'd hit her. Clutching Robbie tightly, she backed away from Drake, her vivid blue eyes wide and startled. "I—I can't give Robbie to you," she said, her voice catching on a gasp. "I won't give him up. He—he's mine!"

"And mine, so you say," Drake said calmly, walking toward her. He was smiling, presumably at the baby, those light blue eyes of his gleaming.

Nicole was incensed. "You're certainly taking this in stride," she accused, continuing to walk backward as Drake proceeded forward. "I've heard of being laid-back but this is ridiculous!"

Drake smiled. "I stand guilty as charged. Yes, I'm laid-back. And you might as well add mellow to the list, too. Nothing upsets me. Drives you high-strung, intense types up the wall, I know."

"I'm not high-strung and intense," Nicole retorted.

"Yes, you are. Nervous, too."

"Well, if you had the sense of a gnat, you'd be nervous yourself right now. How can you be so calm and composed when I've just introduced you to your *son*? Why, it's as if this is nothing out of the ordinary for you, as if it happens to you all the time—*oh*!"

She broke off in horror, casting him a fierce glare. "You're even more of a—a rake and a rat than I thought, Drake Austin. This *has* happened to you before, hasn't it? Being introduced to unknown offspring is probably commonplace to you! How many other deluded young girls have you—"

"Had my wicked way with?" Drake supplied helpfully. He'd backed Nicole against the wall and stood just inches in front of her, their bodies nearly touching.

Robbie crowed and grinned and stretched out his little arms to Drake in invitation.

"He likes me," Drake observed, pleased. "He wants me to hold him."

"Over my dead body!" snapped Nicole. She swiftly sidestepped, holding Robbie tight. Too tight. The baby began to squirm and then vocalized a definite protest.

"If Robbie is my son, we might as well get acquainted," Drake pointed out in a maddeningly reasonable tone of voice. "Since he's going to be living with me, he ought to start getting used to me right away."

"He's not going to be living with you!" cried Nicole. "You can't possibly think I'd ever give him up. I—"

"Ms. Fortune, I don't know what to think. I don't know anything about you at all. How could I, when I've never met you before?"

Nicole stared at him, a sickening anxiety creeping through her. Watching her intently, Drake read the fear in her eyes for what it was.

"It's not going to work, honey," he said softly. "Contrary to what you might've read about me, I'm not the indiscriminate sexual adventurer the popular press has painted me. There are no forgotten women from forgotten one-night stands in my life. I don't have a never-ending parade through my bedroom and never have. I'm well acquainted with every woman I've ever slept with and I've always been very careful not to leave any of them with a little Drake Junior—or a little Robbie, as the case may be."

He reached out to cup her chin in his big hand and tilted her head upward, forcing her to meet his gaze. "I've never met you before today, Nicole Fortune. I've never even seen you before."

His voice was even and calm, without a trace of the fury or scorn she'd been expecting. Which made it all the more difficult for her, she admitted grimly to herself. She'd come prepared to deal with fury and scorn. She was at a loss against his equable logic. Not to mention his touch. The feel of his strong fingers sent disturbing tremors through her.

"If I had met you, I'd have remembered, Nicole," Drake continued, his gaze holding hers. "I have an excellent memory for faces and yours is pretty enough to be memorable in any case. I am not the father of your child and you know it as well as I do."

Her child. Nicole's mouth was dry. Of course he would think that. Hadn't she meant him to? And Robbie was her child in every way that counted! But she'd been crazy to believe that she might pass herself off as one of those forgotten women from one of those forgotten one-night stands he'd just denied ever having. Who would have dreamed that a man like Drake Austin actually kept track of his lovers?

Did that mean he would remember Cheryl? A fine sheen of nervous perspiration broke out on her forehead. He'd just said he was always very careful with his lovers and Nicole knew that was a direct reference to his use of precautions. But how could that be? Cheryl had very definitely named Drake Austin as Robbie's father. And Robbie most certainly existed.

Drake's hand slid to her throat and she felt his fingers move lightly, sensitively along her smooth skin. Nicole was vividly aware of his body heat as he stood so close to her, holding her with just one hand. For a split second she had the strangest longing to sway forward and lean into his hard strength which both beckoned and tempted. To close her eyes and let his strong arms surround her, protect her . . .

And then warning bells sounded an alarm in her head. Was she out of her mind? *She* was the strong one upon whom others depended, Nicole reminded herself. She was the protector and always had been. She couldn't imagine it being any other way. But that unfamiliar momentary impulse to submit to Drake Austin held a powerful appeal. She gazed into his beautiful blue eyes, feeling shaken and dazed.

"Nicole, who is Robbie's father?" Drake asked quietly. "I promise you can trust me with the truth."

Nicole pulled away from him, resisting the urge to run from the office and not come back. She didn't have that luxury, not when Robbie's welfare was at stake. "Robbie's father is Drake Austin," she said stubbornly. Her pulses were beginning to pound and echo in her ears. This wasn't going at all as she'd imagined. Once again she cursed the reckless, impulsive streak in her nature which had sent her here in a fit of outraged anxiety.

"A freshman biology student could take one look at you and me and Robbie and know that I couldn't be the baby's father," Drake said in a placating, almost soothing tone. "It's a biological impossibility. You and I have blue eyes, Nicole. Robbie's eyes are brown. Ever heard of the Mendelian laws of genetics? They state unequivocally that two blue-eyed parents can not produce brown-eyed offspring."

Nicole felt her heart leap into her throat at the same moment her stomach somersaulted. The effects left her simultaneously breathless and queasy. He was right, of course. She remembered freshman biology and Gregor Mendel and inherited traits. Blue eyes were produced by two recessive genes, one from each parent. And Cheryl Graham, her foster sister and Robbie's biological mother, had blue eyes, too. Nicole's knees went suddenly weak and she trembled.

Drake Austin noticed and slipped a supportive arm around her. "Come and sit down," he said solicitously. He tried to lead her over to the sectional sofa in a corner of his office.

Nicole snapped out of her daze in a hurry. "There's a couch in your office?" She stared dubiously at the plush gray cushions. Until she'd seen this one, she couldn't have imagined an office large enough to fit a sofa.

"For all those seductions and affairs I carry on," Drake said dryly. "We rapacious rakes believe in comfort and convenience anytime, anywhere."

Nicole stared at him. She knew he was kidding, that he was poking fun at himself and his outrageous reputation. His smile was wry and ironic and invited her to smile along with him, to join in the joke. But she couldn't. She was too unnerved, by him as well as by this entire situation which was rapidly escalating beyond her control.

She glanced nervously above the couch at the long wide wall covered by innumerable framed photographs. Many were of ads which she'd seen countless times in countless magazines—and a few times in news stories, too. Her eyes lit on the one of the provocative couple in the sexy, controversial jeans ad, then flicked to the stunning blonde in the sexy, notorious lingerie ad before coming to rest on the titillating group of nubile, oiled bodies in the sexy, outrageous—and infamous—perfume ad which had been vociferously banned from a number of "family" magazines.

"If it's true that every picture tells a story, then the lesson here is that blatant sex sells." Once again, her thoughts spilled out as words. Nicole stared at the gallery of models and celebrities he'd photographed, many of them beautiful women flimsily draped or wearing scanty clothing or absolutely nothing at all.

Her eyes widened. The nudes were artful, yet erotic, somehow evoking contrasting moods of intimacy and mystery. Nicole swallowed. Those women had taken off their clothes and lain naked in front of Drake Austin while he photographed them, exposing more than their bare flesh with his camera and his cunning perception. To her consternation, she felt her face flush. She quickly turned away.

"If you're going to lecture me on exploiting sex for commercial purposes, please spare me," Drake said lightly. "I've heard it all before. I don't suppose you'd care to hear my views on photography as an art form, regardless of its mercantile use in advertising. As for the nudes—"

"Never mind the nudes," Nicole interjected quickly. "I'm sure the girlie magazines pay you exorbitant fees for your—your work."

"I don't work for girlie magazines." The irritation in his voice was barely decipherable but was nonetheless a deviation from his perpetual air of light detachment. "My nudes are displayed only in my shows or in my books of photography—which have been very well received, I might add."

Her eyes flashed. "I'm sure. Battalions of dirty old men in raincoats probably slather over them the whole way home from the bookstore."

She looked so indignant, and so utterly sincere. "It's been a long time since anyone has come into my office and not pandered to my ego." Drake chuckled in spite of himself. "But let's call a truce, honey. After all, I held back with the name joke, Miss Fortune. You sort of owe me one."

"I owe you nothing, Drake Austin!"

"Nor do I owe you anything, Nicole." His eyes seemed to bore into hers. "Do I?"

She didn't know what to say, how to answer him. Her teeth closed anxiously over her lower lip and she sank down onto the sofa, Robbie in her arms. Drake sat down beside her and Robbie babbled conversationally, waving his little hands excitedly.

"Do you want to be a model, Nicole?" Drake asked, and when she looked at him, she found him watching her intently. "Is that what this little scene is all about?"

"Me? A model?" she repeated incredulously and then she actually laughed. "You can't be serious! I have about as much chance of being a model as I do being crowned queen of England. Not that I want to be either," she added quickly.

"You're an aspiring photographer, then?"

She shook her head. "I'm perfectly content taking pictures with my old camera and putting them in a photo album."

"Not a week goes by that some ambitious soul doesn't try to get to me to launch their career," Drake said with a shrug. "You wouldn't believe the gimmicks that young hopefuls trying to break into modeling have dreamed up. The would-be photographers are just as aggressive." He shrugged again. "I remarked to Carmen, my secretary, that bringing along a baby was a whole new approach. And accusing me of being its father—well, hey, that assured you of getting in to see me, didn't it, honey?"

"Stop calling me honey," Nicole said crossly. "No, I do not want to be a model or a photographer. The sole reason I came here is because," her voice lowered and the irritation drained away, "because Drake Austin is Robbie's father." She glanced at the blue-eyed man and the brown-eyed baby. "At least I thought he was. I thought you were," she corrected, giving her head a slight shake.

Oh, murder, this was getting muddled, she thought glumly. She couldn't even imagine what he must be thinking about this fiasco.

She stood up abruptly, shifting Robbie to her left hip in an attempt to keep his busy little hands from grabbing her hair again. "But you're right,

You have blue eyes and you couldn't possibly be Robbie's father so I—"

"Wait." Drake's voice was unmistakably commanding. "There are a few questions I want to ask before you leave."

Nicole's heart took off at a frantic pace. "Look, I'm sorry to have disturbed you, but—"

"You thought I was your baby's father," Drake finished for her. "Why did you think that, Nicole?"

Fear began to creep along her spine, making her shiver a little. How could she ever tell him about Cheryl? For the first time since she'd impulsively boarded the bus with Robbie this morning, determined to make Drake Austin face up to his long overdue responsibilities, Nicole began to consider the consequences of her actions.

Drake put his arms on either side of Robbie, placed his hands on her shoulders, and gently but firmly lowered her down onto the cushions. And he didn't remove his hands, keeping them cupped just as as gently and firmly over her slim, bare shoulders. "Nicole, if you won't answer that, then tell me why—"

"Robbie's getting restless," she interjected quickly, trying to mask the desperation she was feeling. On top of that, the strong feel of his big, warm hands on her skin was producing a hot, tingling sensation deep in her belly. Lithely, she wiggled away from him. "We have to go. We have a long bus ride back."

"Back to where?"

She was trembling now. And too shaken to come up with a credible lie. "Newark," she admitted.

"You live in *Newark*?"

"Newark is a great place to live," Nicole replied hotly. "So it gets bad press here in New York City. Well, in Newark, New York gets the bad press."

"Hey, I don't want to start a turf war. I just want to know why you came here today with the baby."

She shot him an impatient glare. "I told you why the moment I set foot in your office."

"That's not the answer I'm looking for," Drake said in that neutrally pleasant tone of his. "Why did you wait until Robbie was nine months old to inform his—er—alleged father of his existence? What circumstances sent you here with him today?"

"Why do you care?" she demanded, her blue eyes darkening with desperation. "You're no longer involved. Your blue eyes are genetic proof that you couldn't possibly be Robbie's father, so— "

"But I believe that you really did think that Drake Austin fathered your baby, Nicole. That means someone told you his name was Drake Austin. And when a man goes around impersonating me—while impregnating a woman—I can't help but feel . . . curious." His expression, pleasant, curious, and calmly detached, never changed.

"How cool you are." Nicole marveled at him in spite of herself. "Most men would be ranting and raving at the thought of having their name used in a deception like this. You certainly are mellow, Drake Austin. Does *anything* bother you, I wonder?"

"Not much." Something flickered in his eyes, but was gone before she could begin to interpret it. "But I do admit to having a certain curiosity about young unmarried mothers who've been deluded and dumped by their babies' fathers."

"Why?" she asked warily.

Drake stood up. For the first time since she'd barged into his office, he actually looked uneasy. Nicole stood up too, staring at him, fascinated. "Why?" she pressed.

For a moment, she thought he wasn't going to answer. She watched his lips twist into a wry, fixed smile. "I guess because my mother was one."

Nicole blinked. "Your mother wasn't married to your father when she had you?"

"How could she be?" Drake asked carelessly.

"He was already married to another woman. Of course he didn't bother to tell her that until it was too late."

"How can you treat it so lightly?" demanded Nicole. "What your father did was terrible! He used your mother, he deceived her. And what about his responsibilities to you? Did he ever fulfill them or did he simply walk away, leaving your mother holding the baby? Literally!"

"And you said you weren't intense." Drake laughed. "Look how you're reacting to a situation from the distant past which doesn't even concern you!"

"A situation that was and is intolerable. You should be upset about it, too!"

"I'm thirty-five years old, Nicole. I can hardly get worked up over anything that happened so long ago."

"And which still affects you to this very day! Does someone ever get over knowing that his father didn't care enough about him to acknowledge him? To marry his mother and give him his name?"

Drake frowned thoughtfully. "Interestingly enough, my father did acknowledge me. Sort of. Although he never paid any child support, it was common knowledge in our town that I was his son. My mother made sure that his name was listed on my birth certificate. Austin is my father's surname."

"Well, my mother wasn't permitted to use my father's name on *my* birth certificate," Nicole said, her blue eyes flashing fire. "He swore her to secrecy and paid her to leave town. Fortune is my mother's surname—the line for 'father' was left blank. To this day my mother won't tell me the weasel's name."

Drake gaped at her. He dropped his laid-back, there's-nothing-that-can-surprise-me demeanor to stare at her, nonplussed. "Are you telling me that your father and your mother weren't married either?"

"It's a weird coincidence, I agree. How old was your mother when she had you?"

"Twenty."

"Mine was seventeen. Just a naive kid." Nicole heaved a sigh. "She's still naive, in an idealistic, optimistic sort of way. She's always dreamed of saving the world and everybody in it. Right now she's working in a refugee camp in Pakistan."

"And you're left alone with a baby. Why did you do it, Nicole? Why did you have a child out of wedlock? You grew up knowing what it was like. . . ."

His voice trailed off. And then he smiled, that mellow, nothing-bothers-me smile. "Not that I'm implying there's anything wrong with it, you understand. My mother's marital status—or the lack of it—and my own position never bothered me. But from what you've said, it sounds as if you weren't too happy under those circumstances."

In that moment, Nicole knew that his casual, laid-back facade was just that. A facade. Drake Austin had cared, all right. She could guess just how much he had cared. Their circumstances were similar enough for her to know the questions and the anger and the hurt that he'd experienced, for she had endured them all, too. But Drake had turned inward, masking his emotions. She hadn't. If anything, her emotions were too close to the surface and she was forever landing in the proverbial soup because of it. Like now . . .

"I—uh—" She stalled for time. He'd called it right, she thought grimly. Having grown up illegitimate and alternately raging at the longing for the father who'd never been there, she would never inflict such pain on a child of hers. But Cheryl hadn't had those compunctions. Cheryl and the man who had called himself Drake Austin had deliberately planned to have a baby without bothering to marry first.

Nicole frowned, remembering Cheryl's tearful confession. It would help if she could tell Drake as much of the truth as possible. "Drake Austin—not you, the bogus one—wanted a child. He didn't exactly promise marriage along with it, but he hinted at it." That's what Cheryl had said, and Nicole had groaned at her gullibility.

Drake grew very still. He stared at Robbie for a long moment, then walked stiffly to his desk. Nicole watched him remove something from a drawer and then return to her side.

"Does he look familiar, Nicole?" He held out a color photograph for her to see.

Nicole stared at it. A young man with dark hair and big, cocoa-brown eyes stared back at her. He was very good-looking, and his smug smile and the gleam in his dark eyes revealed that he knew it.

Nicole disliked him on sight, just as she had the first time she'd seen this very photo—in Cheryl's Book of Hunks. The title was pure Cheryl and Nicole cringed every time she pulled the scrapbook out. Cheryl kept a photographic record of her many conquests. It was rather alarming to see how quickly she added new pages to it. Row after row of handsome men, of all ages, races, and creeds. Cheryl believed in equal opportunity and did not discriminate against any willing man.

Another of Cheryl's quirks was not writing the names of the men in her Book of Hunks album. Sometimes Nicole wondered if she even remembered them. It was an unfortunate omission. Had the men in the scrapbook been identified, she would've known at first glance that the smiling smoothie in this picture was not the Drake Austin into whose office she had charged.

Drake interpreted her silence another way. "You know him," he said flatly. "Don't bother to deny it, Nicole, I've been watching you very closely. I saw the recognition in your eyes the moment you looked at the photograph."

"What's his real name?" Nicole asked quietly.

"Andrew Austin. He's my half brother." Drake drew a sharp breath. "He was killed in a car accident seventeen months ago." He fixed intent blue eyes on Nicole. "You would've been about a month into your pregnancy at that time. But since Andrew hadn't mentioned you to the family, no one knew about you. Or the baby."

Nicole's memory flashed back to Cheryl's tearful announcement of her pregnancy. From the time they'd been children, when Cheryl was in trouble she came to Nicole to get her out of it—and her out-of-wedlock pregnancy definitely qualified as trouble. She remembered that Cheryl had claimed that "Drake Austin" had talked her into getting pregnant and then dropped out of her life. Hoping he would come back, Cheryl had gone through with the pregnancy but "Drake Austin" hadn't reappeared. She was only too relieved to hand baby Robbie over to Nicole and get on with her peripatetic life.

"What kind of a man was your brother, anyway? First he used your name while deliberately trying to father a child, then—" she heaved a sigh and shook her head. "Oh, what's the use of condemning a dead man? Thank you for the information about your brother. It does—explain—some things."

"But you didn't come here for an explanation, you came to insist that Robbie's father contribute to his support," Drake reminded her.

"And I'm sorry I did." Was she ever! She felt as hapless as the mythical Pandora who had opened up that infamous box. Now all she wanted to do was to extricate herself and Robbie from this unfortunate mess.

"I—I didn't realize the circumstances or I'd never have come. Uh, Drake, I'm sorry about your brother's death—you and your family have my deepest sympathy. I'll leave now. You don't ever have to worry about my bothering you again."

Drake fastened his fingers around her wrist as securely as a handcuff. "You're not exactly grief-stricken over Andrew's death," he pointed out.

Nicole swallowed. "No, I'm not," she admitted. She guessed she must sound heartless, but she couldn't play it any other way. She was a terrible actress. Feigning grief over a man who'd supposedly been her lover but whom she in truth had never met would surely challenge the talents of even a budding Meryl Streep.

"Obviously, you didn't love Andrew." Drake's voice was dry and detached again. "And as Andrew seemed incapable of loving anyone but himself, it's probably safe to say that he didn't love you."

Nicole nodded. It was *very* safe to say that. She and Andrew Austin had never laid eyes on each other. She tried to unobtrusively wiggle her wrist free from his grasp. Drake did not release her.

"Drake, I have to leave. Robbie will be getting hungry and—"

The baby interrupted her with a sudden wail. Nicole blessed his impeccable timing. "There it goes—his appetite alarm just sounded. You could set a clock by him." She couldn't seem to stop talking as she tried to make her way to the door.

Unfortunately, she wasn't getting anywhere. Her wrist was still manacled by Drake's unyielding fingers. "I'll send Carmen out to get him something to eat. Tell me what you want for him. And for yourself, too. We might as well all have lunch," Drake commanded genially, but Nicole saw the steely determination in his light blue eyes.

She set her jaw, hoping to appear forcefully authoritative. "I don't want to stay, Drake. We're leaving!" But the booming tones she'd intended came out sounding more like a panicky squeak.

Drake was the epitome of unruffled calm, in stark contrast to her increasing agitation. "If I let you go, you'll disappear," he predicted coolly. "I'll never see or hear from you or Robbie again."

How true, Nicole thought, her heart hammering in her chest. "I—I—" she began, wondering what he wanted to hear. That she and Robbie would stay out of his life forever? Oh, that would be an easy promise to make!

"And I can't let that happen," Drake said, staring down at her, his gaze piercing. "Robbie is my brother's child."

"Your half brother's child," Nicole corrected weakly.

Drake arched his dark brows. "That still makes him my nephew."

"Half nephew," Nicole interjected stubbornly. Half or whole, Robbie was Drake Austin's blood relative. And she wasn't. Her stomach churned with anxiety. Robbie's mother, Cheryl Graham, had been her foster sister, placed at the age of eleven in the Fortune home by the Department of Child Welfare. There was no blood link or adoption papers to legalize the relationship which technically had ended when Cheryl turned eighteen and the agency had relinquished control over her life.

Drake Austin's legal claim on the child was irrefutable; hers tenuous at best. Nicole blanched, then forced herself to shake off the terrible thought. Why should Drake Austin display anything more than a detached, semiavuncular interest in a child he'd never heard of until today?

"I can see you're upset, Nicole," Drake said soothingly, his thumb absently stroking the finely veined skin on the inside of her wrist. Nicole's nerves, already clamoring, suddenly seemed to speed into overdrive.

"Relax, there's nothing to worry about. I didn't mean to alarm you." His voice, smooth as honey, flowed over her. "But it's necessary that you stay and talk with me for a while. As Robbie's mother, you're entitled to know everything about his inheritance."

He dropped her wrist and took the squirming baby from her arms. "If you came here because of money problems—and I assume that you did—then all your worries are over, Nicole. As Andrew's heir, your son is going to be quite a rich little fellow."

Two

In a melodrama she would sink into a faint at such an announcement, Nicole thought irrelevantly, striving to appear calm. Robbie, rich? The notion was terrifying. A large inheritance would induce Drake Austin to maintain an active interest in his half brother's child.

And wouldn't the team of lawyers which undoubtedly oversaw the distribution of said large inheritance want proof of Robbie's parentage? They would want his birth certificate and blood tests—proof that he was an Austin. The tests would prove the infant's paternity, all right. Just as they would reveal that she was not Robbie's mother!

She would lose Robbie. Drake Austin or any member of the Austin family could legally take him away from her! For a moment, Nicole felt she really was going to faint.

Drake looked at her whitened face, his brows narrowing with concern. "Nicole, are you all right?"

Nicole stared at him, holding Robbie, and felt a rush of emotion sweep through her. "No, I'm not all right," she cried. "I didn't bring Robbie here to be anyone's heir! I just wanted—"

"What did you want, Nicole?" Drake asked, interrupting. He was watching her, an unreadable expression on his face. "Are you finally going to tell me what prompted you to seek out Robbie's father today?"

Nicole ran her hand nervously through her hair, tousling it. It was no use being evasive on that issue. He obviously wasn't going to let it drop. "I guess it really began six months ago when my sister Hailey's husband walked out on her. They'd been having problems for years, but she was determined to make the marriage work so she overlooked his gambling and his drinking. . . . But she couldn't overlook his heading for the West Coast with his teenage girlfriend and his last paycheck."

"Understandably," Drake agreed dryly.

"Anyway, Hailey was left with their three children and no money. The rent was already in arrears and since she couldn't come up with the payment, she was evicted. She and the kids moved in with us."

"Your sister and her three children are living with you and Robbie? In Newark?"

"What offends you more?" Nicole demanded, immediately on the defensive. "The fact that Hailey and the children are living with us or that we're living in Newark?"

Drake hid a smile. "I'm not offended by either," he assured her. "So you decided that since you had four extra mouths to feed, it was about time that Robbie's father kicked in his share of child support?"

"No." Nicole scowled. "It was tight, but I was managing. I have a good job but—"

"You have a job?" Drake interrupted.

He was obviously surprised to hear it. Nicole burned. "Yes, I have a job. How do you think we live? Do you think we depend on the 'kindness of strangers'?" Under the circumstances, he probably did. And he could hardly be faulted for it. She reined in her temper. "I'm a high school teacher—

the school where I teach is just a block away from where we live so it's very convenient."

"What do you teach?" She looked so young, not long out of high school herself, he thought.

"Home Arts—that's cooking, sewing, and a unit called marriage and family. Two years ago, I started a day nursery for children three and under right there at the school, so I take Robbie along with me."

"Why do you have a day nursery in a high school?" Drake wanted to know.

"It's for the students' children. So many of them have them. I began a child development course and the nursery is a kind of living lab. There's been a definite, positive effect on both the mothers and the babies in the program."

Drake frowned thoughtfully. "Children having children. There's been a lot of that in the media lately."

"The media picks up topics and drops them just as quickly when something new comes along," Nicole noted dryly. "At Robert Kennedy High School, we live with the reality of children having children." She sighed softly. "School will let out for summer vacation in two weeks and I worry about the kids—all of them, the mothers and the little ones on their own, all day. . . ." Her voice trailed off as she thought of the long, hot summer ahead.

"Does the school term ending have an effect on your financial situation?" persisted Drake.

Nicole forced her thoughts back to the here and now. "No. The problem arose when I took Robbie to the pediatrician for his well-baby checkup this morning. The doctor said—"

"Is there something wrong with the baby?" There wasn't a trace of his laid-back, casual attitude in Drake's exclamation of concern.

"No, no. It's nothing very serious. But the doctor said that both Robbie's feet are turning inward. To correct it, he prescribed these special shoes to be worn night and day for about a year. They're white leather with rigid, thick soles and keep the feet completely straight. The doctor said they're a lot like the traditional high-top baby shoes, except they look like they're on the wrong feet."

She paused for a breath, then plunged ahead. "And they cost almost seventy-five dollars a pair. Since he'll be wearing them to bed, as well as all day, he'll need at least two pairs—and he's growing so fast, he'll need several more pairs if he's to wear them a whole year!"

She drew a deep breath. "I knew I couldn't afford it, not with the additional expense of Hailey and her kids living with us. I felt so helpless and—and enraged, too. My baby needed shoes and I couldn't get them for him and manage to keep up with our everyday living expenses."

She grimaced, remembering her desperation—and her fury. "It just struck me as so unfair—how men can absent themselves from their children's lives and get away with it. The mothers are left with sole responsibility for raising the children, physically, emotionally, and financially."

"Like you and Robbie living out the same scenario that you and your mother did," Drake said perceptively. "And your sister and her children as well. I know exactly how you feel. I felt it, too, all those years that my mother struggled to support me while my father's three legal sons lived in luxury on the other side of town."

The words were out before he could censor himself. Drake wanted to recall them immediately. He couldn't, of course, but he could negate them. He forced a wordly smile, emoting an air of total sangfroid. "I was the poor little poor boy and they were the classic spoiled little rich boys. A boringly predictable conflict."

"I don't think it's boring." Nicole looked at him,

momentarily riveted. "You actually knew all about your half brothers when you were a child?"

"Oh yes. Andrew was just a year younger than I. The other boys, Dane and Ian, were four and five years younger. My father introduced me to them when I was ten, but I'd learned about them years before from my mother. She used to take me to their house and we'd stand on the sidewalk and watch the boys playing in their yard."

Now what had prompted him to tell her that? he wondered, startled by how easily he'd confided in her. No one who knew him considered him to be introspective and insightful. He kept those aspects of his private self hidden, preferring to relate to others with a light, glib style that precluded intimacy.

"Your childhood sounds as strange as mine," Nicole said with a wry smile. "My mother didn't want me to grow up as an only child, but she didn't want to get involved with another man to have another baby either, so she took in foster children. Kids were coming and going all the time at our house—you never knew when you left for school in the morning who would be there when you came back in the afternoon. A few of the kids were long-term placements and stayed with us until they were grown—Hailey was one of them. We're the same age and have been best friends from the time she came to live with us when we were both nine."

"And now she's back living with you—along with her kids. Kind of an instant replay of your childhood. People unpredictably coming and going."

Neither he nor Nicole had exactly lived the idyllic childhood portrayed on *Leave it to Beaver*, he mused with a half smile. Maybe that was the reason why he found it easy to talk so freely with her about his past when he'd always avoided mention of it to anyone else.

"I'm glad to help Hailey and the kids," Nicole

said fiercely. "What upset me was not being able to go out and buy Robbie those shoes. And then I happened to think of an article I'd read about you in a magazine, how you were so successful and owned a big house in the Hamptons and an apartment in New York and a zillion cars. I just blew up. Remember, I thought you were Robbie's father then. And I figured that the least you could do for your own child was to buy him a few pairs of special shoes."

"So you took Robbie to the Newark bus station and here you are," Drake finished for her.

"It was stupid of me. I acted before I thought things through."

"Which, I'd hazard a guess, isn't unusual for you," Drake said with an amused smile.

Nicole was not amused. No, it wasn't unusual, but this time the results could prove disastrous. "You can have Robbie's money," she said quickly, desperately. "We don't need it. Just give me my baby and let us alone."

"You don't need it? What about the baby's shoes? And aren't your sister and her children still living with you?"

Nicole nodded. Robbie caught her eye and beamed at her and she felt a rush of hot tears prick her eyes. She couldn't lose him. She wouldn't! She began to inch closer to the door. The sooner she could escape from his office the better.

"Then you certainly need financial assistance, Nicole. Nothing's changed since you boarded that bus this morning."

Everything had changed, she silently contradicted. She continued to stealthily move toward the door and freedom.

About lunch . . ." Drake watched her slow, subtle progression to the door. Impossibly enough, it seemed as if she wanted to bolt from his office. And she'd definitely seemed distressed to hear about the money that a child of Andrew Austin was legally entitled to. He couldn't figure her out. She'd come here to demand financial support for her child from its father, a principle that he could fully understand. And champion. Yet the moment he'd mentioned Robbie's sizable inheritance, she'd had an abrupt change of heart.

She looked up at him and caught him staring at her. Their eyes met and held. Nicole clung to Robbie, feeling vulnerable under Drake's steady, unblinking gaze. Once again she felt herself involuntarily responding to that much-heralded sexual magnetism of his. Hot little tendrils of sensation pierced her abdomen and darted lower.

Her pulses raced with alarm as well as arousal. Drake Austin was totally out of her reach, out of her class and her financial bracket. And right now he was her most dangerous adversary. If he were ever to learn that Cheryl was Robbie's real mother . . .

Nicole felt her heart stop, then start again with a jarring thud. He would take Robbie away from her, she knew he would. She quickly turned away from him, giving her full attention to the baby, who was babbling an incomprehensible string of syllables in a definite tone of complaint.

Drake was indulging in a few mental machinations of his own. He was too experienced not to have recognized for exactly what it was the flicker of sexual awareness which had flared in her deep blue eyes. He watched her quickly drop her gaze in an attempt to conceal what he had seen there, studying her as she turned her attention to the baby in her arms.

Drake stared at the mother and child, at Andrew's son in the arms of Andrew's lover. Odd, but he would've never picked Nicole Fortune for one of Andrew's women. She wasn't his type, not at all. Andrew had invariably favored flamboyant blondes, the brighter their hair the better, their tiny minds in direct inverse proportion to their large mammaries. Andrew's women giggled a lot and were easy and compliant, nothing at all like this slender brunette whose startlingly vivid blue eyes were alert with intelligence and intensity.

And then strangely, and totally against his will, Drake felt his body tighten with the stirrings of arousal. He tried to drag his eyes away from her, but they seemed to be operating of their own volition, returning to stare at Nicole, compulsively, intently.

His photographer's eye noted that her face was a bit too angular to be considered beautiful and her features were not the classic ones of the models he photographed for magazine covers and high-fashion layouts. Her eyes were striking: big, piercingly blue, and wide-set, but her nose was a bit too small and her mouth a bit too wide, her lower lip sensually full. Her hair was too long and too straight, not permed, crimped, moussed, or spritzed in the latest fashionable cut.

But there was something about her. . . . Put together, her uneven features created an interesting, exotic look which exerted an appeal all her own. Her face was animated and expressive. One felt compelled to watch her so as not to miss the mercurial changes of her mouth, the quick tilt of her head, the glowing intensity in her eyes.

Accustomed to working with almost anorexically thin models, Drake let his eyes linger appreciatively on the rounded feminine curves of her figure, the sweet breasts, the slim waist, and gentle flare of her hips. The skirt of her bright sundress came to the top of her knee, revealing legs that were shapely—and bare. It was June and the temperature was in the eighties, and she'd done without hose.

Nor was she wearing a bra. The thin straps and fitted bodice of her sundress precluded one. Almost compulsively, Drake's eyes again settled on her breasts. He'd never cared for the silicone enormities of Andrew's women. Nicole's breasts, firm and full beneath the cotton sundress, looked as though they would fit his palms perfectly. He found himself wondering about the size and shape of her nipples and felt his body grow hard.

Abruptly, he took refuge behind his desk, sinking into his chair with a dizzying feeling of disorientation. What was happening to him? he wondered as he buzzed Carmen over the intercom. He was famed for his legendary cool, but he wasn't feeling mellow or laid-back now. He felt hot and restless and totally disconcerted. He was used to working with the world's most beautiful women and retaining his composure, yet staring at Nicole Fortune had aroused him faster and harder than ever before.

And it was wrong, all wrong. He wasn't about to become involved with his half brother's lover, with the mother of Andrew's child. He wasn't going to allow the sick competitive streak which had consumed Andrew affect him, too.

And in simpler, less psychological terms, Nicole Fortune just wasn't his type, not any more than she'd been Andrew's. She was too intense and emotional, and intense emotions were anathema to Drake Austin. He doubted that casual and mellow were even in her vocabulary and they were the cornerstones of his personality. Worst of all, she was undoubtedly commitment-prone and he was commitment-phobic.

Carmen entered the office, carrying a heavy canvas tote bag. "You left this in the reception area," she said, handing it to Nicole. "I thought you might need it for the baby."

"I do, thanks," said Nicole. "He's ready for his lunch."

"Do you breastfeed him?" Drake asked in an oddly strangled tone of voice. He pictured her lowering the straps and bodice of her dress and offering her nipple to the baby. A rush of blood pooled heavily in his groin.

"Not with those teeth of his she doesn't," Carmen interjected humorously.

Nicole was grateful for her presence. The silence in the office had become so charged and tense that her palms had begun to sweat, despite the cooling air-conditioning. She told herself that she was afraid of Drake Austin because of what he could do to her and Robbie, but she knew that wasn't the only reason. He also made her aware of herself and her femininity in a way she had never experienced before. He stirred dangerous feelings inside her, feelings she had no business having for a rich, sophisticated heartbreaker like Drake Austin.

They were a billion light years apart in attitude, in philosophy, in station in life, in everything! Their worlds would normally have never touched, but for this temporary collision, brought about by her own impulsive flash of temper.

"I have a jar of strained peaches and one of chicken for Robbie's lunch," Nicole said, directing her remarks to Carmen and carefully avoiding Drake Austin's magnetic blue eyes. "I guess I'd better feed him before I leave."

She knew she couldn't delay his lunch a minute longer. Robbie was vociferously attacking the canvas tote with his small hands.

Carmen smiled. "I guess you'd better. He's not about to be put off. Can I hold him for you while you get his things out?"

Nicole gratefully handed over the baby and proceeded to remove a large bib, a plastic spoon and two small jars of strained food. And she almost dropped them all when Drake spoke up: "Carmen, cancel everything I have scheduled today. I'm driving Ms. Fortune and the baby back to Newark."

"Oh no, there's no need to do that!" Nicole exclaimed breathlessly. "Robbie and I will take the bus. I wouldn't dream of disrupting your schedule. I know how busy you must be!"

Drake smiled dryly. "My schedule is of little consequence now, Nicole. You've disrupted my *life*. As for taking the bus back to Newark, forget it. I'm taking you and Robbie back, and that's final. I want to see where you're living with my brother's child and to make arrangements for—"

"No!" cried Nicole. "No to everything, Drake Austin."

An uneasy silence descended. Carmen was the first to break it. "Your brother's child?" she said to Drake. "This is Andrew's baby?"

Drake nodded. "Remember my father's scheme? I laughed it off, but obviously Andrew took it seriously."

Carmen nodded, and Nicole saw the knowing look which passed between Drake and his secretary.

"What scheme?" Nicole dared to ask. She knew she wasn't going to like the answer.

Drake shrugged, that oddly detached smile hovering around the corners of his mouth. "Our father was getting tired of waiting for an heir. He let it be known that his firstborn grandchild would inherit a sizable chunk of his estate—and if the child were a boy, there would be a generous cash settlement paid at his birth to the proud father. Andrew was determined to win the prize."

And so he'd talked Cheryl, a woman he'd picked up in a singles bar, into getting pregnant? Nicole grimaced. Cheryl had confided the tale of their meeting, how "Drake," alias Andrew Austin, had "swept her off her feet." There'd been no mention of cash-on-delivery, though. Apparently Andrew Austin had correctly gauged Cheryl's fervid romantic streak which couldn't have accommodated such a cold-blooded plan. According to Cheryl, the couple had begun their quest for conception an hour after their initial meeting because they'd fallen instantaneously in love.

But that was Cheryl for you, Nicole thought, stifling a weary sigh. All a man had to do to get her into bed was ask. Apparently, that extended to bearing a child as well.

She raised troubled eyes to Drake, who was watching her. He always seemed to be watching her with those enigmatic blue eyes. She quickly turned to Robbie, draping him in the long plastic bib before beginning to shovel strained peaches and junior chicken into his mouth.

"Did Andrew mention anything about the money to you?" Drake asked casually.

"What?" For a moment, Nicole forgot that she was supposed to be the woman Andrew Austin had impregnated—for his own profit. She shuddered with disgust. What a creep Andrew Austin had been! And what a bimbo Drake Austin must think *she* was! It went against every grain of her pride to play such a role. But if she didn't . . . if she were to let it slip that she wasn't the woman who'd given birth to Robbie, she would lose him. She was certain of it.

Concentrating on holding Robbie on her lap while feeding him and keeping him from grabbing the spoon from her, she replied tautly, "This is the first time I've heard any mention of such a plan." That much was true, at least. "And it's the stupidest plan I've ever heard of," she couldn't resist adding. "Only a vain megalomaniac would offer a cash bribe for a grandchild. And only a mercenary idiot would take him up on it."

"A rather accurate assessment of my father and brother Andrew, I'm afraid," Drake said wryly. "But our father did offer the—incentive—which motivated Andrew to sire a child." His gazed focused on Robbie who was eagerly gobbling his lunch.

"If you'll excuse me, I have to get back to my desk," interjected Carmen and swiftly absented herself from the office.

Nicole wished she could escape from this increasingly appalling discussion as easily and efficiently as the secretary had.

"Robbie really seems to like that stuff," Drake remarked, watching Nicole deftly hold and feed the baby.

She was a good mother, he decided thoughtfully. Protective, nurturing, and warm. He found it fascinating to watch her interactions with the baby. She was attuned and responsive to everything Robbie did, and the child seemed equally attuned and responsive to his mother. It was an appealing sight. He hadn't closely observed a mother and her baby before and his objective photographer's eye visualized a whole series of wonderful candid shots of the two of them sitting there on the couch.

Drake watched Nicole's lips part unconsciously as she held the spoon to the baby's lips, and a flare of heat spread from his abdomen and went straight to his head. He wasn't reacting to her as an impartial photographic observer now. His response was that of a man to a desirable woman. But there was more to it than that, he realized with a chill of alarm. He felt drawn to her in a way that he couldn't fully explain to himself, yet he knew it had something to do with her love and loyalty to her baby.

For the first time he was personally aware of the potent appeal of a pretty young woman with a child. He'd shot countless ads featuring women and children which were based on that very attraction: Both the marketing and advertising fields knew that like sex, mothers and babies "sold." The heartwarming pitch had never had any effect on him, however, probably because he was only professionally involved, photographing models who merely simulated what Nicole and Robbie were in reality.

But some primal, masculine instincts were definitely stirring within him now. He felt inexplicably protective toward the young mother and her infant. Possessive somehow.

And then he thought of Andrew, who'd deliberately sought out this woman to produce the son to ensure his fortune. Fortune. That was her name. Was that why Andrew had gone against type and chosen her as mother for his heir? Andrew had always had a dark, perverse sense of humor.

Drake's face hardened. Andrew hadn't been the only one involved, however. The inevitable question of why Nicole had gone to bed with his brother and borne his child bedeviled him. She'd already admitted that she didn't love Andrew. She'd hardly reacted at all to the news of his death. And there was another, equally unsettling question which nagged at him as well. Was she really unaware of the sizable settlement that producing Robbie would bring? And if she knew, why go through the charade of not wanting the money? Could she be trying to pull off a hustle so slick that even he, Drake Austin, with his superlative street smarts, was in danger of being taken in?

Robbie finished his lunch and Nicole laid him on the sofa for a diaper change. She was nervously aware of Drake's silent scrutiny. Once again, she heartily regretted this impromptu trip to his office. Why, why, why had she acted on impulse? She stifled a groan. Set that refrain to music and it could be her theme song.

She removed a bottle of baby formula from her bag and Robbie squealed with pleasure and snatched it from her. He lay back on the sofa, his bare little feet in the air and carried the nipple to his mouth. Nicole smiled warmly at the baby. "He likes to hold his bottle himself now. He'll only let me hold him and give him the bottle at night, before he goes to bed."

Drake's heart turned queerly in his chest. When she smiled in that certain way . . . The warmth and tenderness in her beautiful eyes evoked a startling and wholly inexplicable corresponding warmth and tenderness within him.

God, what was happening to him? he wondered in alarm. This girl affected him as no one ever had before. He was melting under her charms as fast as a marshmallow in a campfire—and he knew very well that she wasn't even trying to be charming! Should she ever decide to really turn it on for him . . . Why, he'd be lost!

"We'll need to have legal proof that Andrew is Robbie's father, of course," he said gruffly, determined to shake the peculiar hold she seemed to have over him. "I'm sure that my father will be delighted to have a grandson at last, but I know he'll want to see Robbie's birth certificate and any other evidence you have proving he's Andrew's child."

"I don't have any evidence proving he's Andrew's child," Nicole said quickly. And that, she thought with relief, was that. "As for his birth certificate, I—I left the line for the father's name blank. Just like on my own birth certificate."

It was a lie, as she well knew. But a necessary one, she assured herself.

"You said his full name was Robert Richard Austin," Drake challenged.

"It is. But his father's name isn't listed on his birth certificate."

"For God's sake, why not?"

Nicole shrugged. "Because it's not."

"Because it's not? *Because*? That's your answer?" Cool, mellow Drake was anything but cool or mellow now. "You'd deny your child his inheritance—*because*!"

Nicole shrugged laconically. "That's right."

"This is crazy! I'm beginning to think that you're crazy! You came here, believing I was Robbie's father, to demand that I contribute to his support, but you didn't bring any evidence that he was Drake Austin's child? Did you expect me merely to take your word for it?"

"I told you I acted impulsively," she reminded him calmly. They seemed to have temporarily switched temperaments. Now she was the unruffled, reasonable one, and he the emotional hothead. "I told you I didn't think it through. You seemed to find it rather amusing a bit earlier."

"Yeah, well, I'm no longer amused. Nor will my father be. He'll accuse you of trying to bilk Andrew's estate by fabricating your child's paternity."

"That's understandable. Why should he believe me? And why do *you* believe that Robbie is Andrew's child without a shred of evidence?"

A logical question, one that his father Preston Austin would be sure to pose, Drake knew. Unfortunately, he had no logical explanation for the primal gut instinct which told him that Andrew was the baby's father. And since he'd spent his life trusting his instincts and hadn't gone wrong yet, he wasn't into second-guessing himself.

"Robbie looks like he was cloned from the baby pictures I've seen of Andrew." He wasn't about to inform Nicole of his faultless intuition. She'd undoubtedly laugh herself silly. "And his age is right, too. He'd have been conceived within a month of our father's bribe, when Andrew was out scouting for a baby-maker."

Nicole winced. Andrew had gone scouting for a baby-maker and found gullible, eager-to-please Cheryl. Poor Cheryl, who had been a sitting duck for so many men's hidden agendas. Her expression hardened. "I'm not going to keep arguing the point with you, Drake. You should be relieved that you and your family are off the hook, legally and financially. I don't intend to make any claims on any of you."

She was right, he *should* be feeling relieved, thought Drake. Instead, he was enraged. "I know that baby is Andrew's child," he said, his color rising to match the anger in his voice. "Robbie is an Austin. You know it, too, Nicole. And it's damn selfish of you to deny him his paternity and his inheritance for—"

"Would your father accept him as an Austin without any evidence?" Nicole interrupted. Words were unnecessary. Drake's expression answered her question. "Well, then, I'm not denying Robbie anything, am I? I'm merely sparing all of us from an unpleasant legal confrontation that Robbie and I couldn't possibly hope to win."

She'd scored another point, which only served to exacerbate the storm of emotions surging through him. Drake began to pace his office. He hadn't experienced this explosive combination of fury and frustration since . . . since he'd been a kid enduring Andrew's unending taunts about not being a "real" Austin. He'd learned long ago to block out anything with the power to rouse his emotions, but this situation touched a raw nerve, exposing feelings he'd thought were dead and buried.

Here was another little boy, a flesh-and-blood Austin, being denied his birthright. It didn't matter that Andrew had never ceased tormenting Drake about his inferior status within the Austin clan, and that Robbie was Andrew's son. Drake couldn't hold his half brother's malice against this innocent child.

Robbie finished his bottle and sleepily rubbed his eyes with his plump baby fists. Nicole picked him up, then crossed the room to stand before Drake. "Drake, I do appreciate your believing me. A lot of people wouldn't have, I know. They'd've tossed me out of the office in three seconds flat. And I appreciate your concern over Robbie's inheritance, but I'm just not prepared in any way to fight your father for a stake of Andrew's money."

Impulsively, she laid her hand on his arm. "Don't worry about us. We'll get by, I promise."

She felt the hard, muscled strength of him beneath her fingers and a bolt of sensual electricity flashed through her. He was close, too close, and she could feel the heat emanating from his big, masculine frame. When she inhaled, the clean male scent of him filled her nostrils. Her senses reeled under the twin potent forces of attraction and arousal, neither of which she wanted to acknowledge. But which were definitely there and couldn't be denied.

Touching him had been a major mistake, Nicole conceded dizzily. Another one. She seemed to have cornered the market on impulsive mistakes today.

Immediately, instinctively, Drake trapped her hand under his own. His body began to throb as an unwelcome surge of heat suffused him once again. It seemed to be a reflexive response to her nearness and he almost backed away from her in pure self-defense. Almost.

But he didn't. He was as mesmerized as she by the compelling sensual aura enveloping them. "I'm not going to let you merely get by," he said huskily. "Whether you have material evidence or not, I know that Robbie is my nephew and—"

His voice trailed off. It was difficult to talk when she was staring at him with those intense blue eyes of hers. His brain clouded. All he could think of was the sweet shape of her mouth, the temptingly sensual fullness of her lower lip. He wanted to touch her, taste her. . . .

He knew it was insane but if he didn't kiss her, he was certain that *he* would go insane.

The vibrations humming between them were too forceful to ignore, though Nicole determinedly tried. "If you want to do something nice for your—your—nephew, you could buy him his first pair of those—"

The words caught in her throat as Drake's other hand settled on her waist to draw her slowly, inexorably closer. A thick, sweet languor suffused her as she watched his head lower to hers. She fought the nearly overpowering need to close her eyes and lift her mouth to his. And lost.

Their lips were only centimeters apart when little Robbie suddenly began to cry. At once, the sensuous spell was irrevocably broken. Nicole jerked away, aghast at the near kiss. The delicious lassitude which flowed through her had left her alarmingly weak. She glanced at Drake furtively through lowered lashes to find him watching her intently. Her every nerve ending seemed to tingle. He was too good-looking, too sexy, too appealing, she remonstrated with herself. And way too dangerous. *Stop looking at him. Get away from him. Now.*

"You really are a smooth operator," she accused, her eyes flashing blue fire. Part of her recognized that the powerful feelings coursing through her needed an outlet. Anger was a convenient one. And emotional distance could be as effective as actual physical distance. "Do you routinely come on to every woman who walks through your door? No, don't bother to answer that, now I *know* you do. And you even have a—a rogues' gallery of your conquests!"

"Are you accusing me of sleeping with every woman I've photographed?" Drake was just as roused as she, and her hostility converted his emotions into an equally convenient burst of anger.

"Yes! You even mount them on your wall—just like a big game hunter mounts his safari trophies! Well, I'm not going to be one of them, Drake Austin!"

"You're damn right, honey. As a photographer, you couldn't afford me. And as a man—"

"I don't want you," she lashed out.

Drake surveyed her lazily, his brief flash of anger gone. "Oh, but you do, baby." His smile was cool and sardonic. "You were as ready and willing as I was. I know hungry eyes when I see them and yours were practically eating me up."

She could've pointed out that those pale blue eyes of his had been equally ravenous as they feasted on her, but she was too infuriated to toss off a metaphorical comeback. She settled Robbie more comfortably in her arms and he lay heavily against her, his big brown eyes drifting shut on a final wail.

"You're a creep, Drake Austin," she hissed in a whisper, so as not to disturb the baby. "And from what you've told me, you come from a long line of creeps. I'm delighted to save Robbie from falling in with the likes of you."

Grabbing her canvas bag, Nicole stormed from the office, leaving the door open. She didn't trust herself not to slam it off its hinges if she touched it and she didn't want to startle Robbie.

She had to pass through Drake's secretary's office to get to the open reception area beyond. "Er, shall I call for Mr. Austin's car to be brought around?" Carmen asked tentatively as Nicole stalked by.

"Not on my account," Nicole replied with as much civility as she could muster. As furious as she might be with Drake Austin, she had no gripe with his secretary. "Robbie and I are taking the bus."

Carmen stood up, her gaze darting from Nicole and the baby to the open door of Drake's office. "Do you have enough for bus fare?" she asked solicitously.

"Yes, thank you." Nicole inclined her head proudly. "Good-bye."

The moment she left Carmen's small office, Drake burst into it. "What a conniving little piranha she is." The devil-may-care laugh he'd intended came out sounding like a snarl instead. "Miss Fortune. She's appropriately named, all right. It's guaranteed misfortune for anyone who crosses her path."

"Is she planning a messy suit against Andrew's estate?" Carmen asked curiously. "Should you warn your father to get in touch with his lawyers? Drake, do you really believe that the baby is Andrew's?"

"He's Andrew's son, I'm sure of it." Carmen tactfully didn't ask why. "But she says she doesn't have any proof that Andrew is the father, not even a birth certificate," he continued with a grimace. "And she claims she doesn't want any money from the Austins."

"Am I missing something here? Are you saying that she's not Miss Fortune-hunter, after all?" Carmen looked puzzled. "Then why is she a conniving little piranha?"

Drake scowled. His insides were still churning from that close encounter in his office. Nicole Fortune had aroused him and then accused him of deliberately trying to seduce her! The unfairness of it all rankled him more than it should, he knew. He, Drake Austin, who never lost his cool, had definitely lost it there. And, though he was doing his best to recoup, it was still lost.

"Because she is, that's why." If Nicole could resort to such verbal idiocy, then so could he, he told himself loftily.

Carmen arched her brows. "I see."

"She expects me to go chasing after her, I'm sure," Drake growled. "Well, she's in for a big surprise! I have no intention of hightailing it after her."

Carmen punched a few buttons on the phone. "Hello, Quigley?" she spoke into the phone. "Bring Mr. Austin's car to the front of the building, please."

"What are you doing? I just said I wasn't going after her. And I'm not! Tell Quigley to keep the car in the garage!" Drake strode purposefully into his office.

Ten minutes later, he was back in Carmen's office. "Tell Quigley to get the car."

"He's waiting out front for you now." Carmen smiled sweetly. "I didn't cancel the order." Her smile broadened. "I'm not a gambling woman but I would've bet a year's salary that you'd go after that girl." Her dark eyes gleamed with humor. "I've worked for you for five years and I've never seen anyone get under your skin the way Nicole Fortune did. Your usual reaction to anything, *anything*, is a shrug and a quip. Nonchalance bordering on indifference. But not with her and that baby."

Drake stared sheepishly at the floor. "It's not her at all," he insisted. "It's the kid. I mean, he's just a little baby and—and *she's* planning to take him to the bus station in the middle of Newark. That's hardly a safe place for an infant."

"Mmm-hmmm." Carmen didn't bother to conceal her mirth. "So it's Uncle Drake to the rescue."

"Exactly," Drake said righteously and headed out the door.

Three

Drake caught up with Nicole as she trudged through the Newark bus terminal. Robbie was sound asleep in her arms and the canvas bag hung heavily on her shoulder. She looked young and tired and vulnerable, and his heart lurched at the sight of her. His characteristic nonchalance disappeared on the spot.

"Where in the hell have you been?" he demanded, positioning himself directly in front of her to block her path. "For the past hour, I've been running around like a lunatic, meeting every freaking bus from New York."

Nicole stared at him. "Why?"

Such a simple question. Drake was incensed that he couldn't come up with an answer to it. *"Because,"* he snapped. "That's why." He disentangled the heavy canvas strap from her and hoisted the tote onto his own shoulder. "Let's go."

She didn't move. He gripped her elbow with his hand and attempted to propel her forward. "I'm driving you home, Nicole. In one of my *zillion* cars," he added caustically.

"I thought we'd said everything there was to say to each other back in your office."

She was unsettled by the sight of him, by the

excitement streaking through her. Knowing he was dangerous, knowing that only trouble could come of any association with him, she was still attracted, fascinated beyond her will, and it unnerved her.

One of her foster brothers, Jerome, sprang quickly to mind. She'd heard Jerome describe the allure that fire held for him in almost those same terms. And his unhealthy attraction had led him to no good end, she reminded herself severely. She would do well to remember Jerome and his ten-year sentence for arson whenever she felt tempted to start something with Drake Austin.

"Your trip here was wasted, Drake. I'm not going with you."

"You will," he said with a determinedly pleasant smile, "even if I have to pick you up and carry you out of here. I don't make empty threats, Nicole, so don't push me."

She tossed her head, her eyes snapping. "I wouldn't advise making any threats—empty or otherwise—to me, Drake Austin. You're not used to dealing with someone like me. I'm not one of those pitifully thin models with their useless little toothpick arms. I'm strong. If you touch me, I'll send you flying through this bus station like a Frisbee."

Drake laughed. He couldn't help himself. "You really have me scared, Nicole. In another minute, I'll run away screaming."

She scowled up at him. "You don't believe I can take care of myself? And my baby?"

His smile was deceptively languid. His light blue eyes shone like polished gems. "You don't believe I can overpower you? With one hand tied behind my back?"

It was a stalemate. They stood staring at each other, neither moving, both determined not to be the first to yield.

It occurred to Drake that he was beginning to

enjoy himself. "You know, I don't remember ever being physically challenged—let alone threatened —by a girl," he drawled. "I'm half tempted to take you up on it."

"If you only knew how many poor suckers have said that to me." Nicole smiled smugly. "Every one of them ended up regretting it mightily. And I'm not a girl," she added. "I'm twenty-four years old, which is years away from girlhood."

"You've given me a terrific lead-in, honey. Which script do you want to follow? The one where I tell you that you're very much a woman in my eyes? Or maybe the one where I demand proof that you're a woman and not a nervous little girl? Both ultimately lead to the same thing." He traced the line of her jaw with one long finger and raised his eyebrows suggestively. "Is that what you're looking for, after all?"

Nicole quickly stepped back from him. Her skin tingled along the path he'd touched. To her acute mortification, she was blushing. "I don't play your scripted little games, Mr. Austin," she said coldly. "And I resent your insulting sexist—"

"Let's not forget chauvinistic," interrupted Drake. "So you're a card-carrying feminist, Ms. Fortune? Imagine my surprise!"

"I'm not a card-carrying feminist. I got thrown out of the women's political action group that I joined," Nicole confessed. "I kept telling them that their agenda was stupid and superfluous and they got sick of me."

"You're a feminist *reject*?"

"My primary concern is for good day care, easily available day care, affordable day care. The chief honchos didn't want to hear it. All they wanted to talk about was why women weren't CEO's of the Fortune Five Hundred companies."

"No pun intended," drawled Drake.

Nicole rolled her eyes. "Sure, make jokes. Meanwhile, there are millions of little kids with working mothers who sweat out child care arrangements every day. And—"

"Please! Put away the soapbox, Nicole." He gave his head a shake. "I begin to understand why you were kicked out of the group. You were probably relentless, grim, and humorless while you pounded your points into all the frustrated CEO wanna-bes."

"The situation *is* relentless and grim," retorted Nicole. "And I defy you to find any humor in small children being left alone all day or in substan—"

"We're digressing," Drake inserted swiftly. "You seem to have a talent for it. Are you going to let me drive you home or are we going to fight it out right here in the Newark bus terminal?"

Nicole heaved an exasperated sigh. "Why won't you just leave us alone? Haven't I made myself clear? Go away!"

"Put yourself in my place, Nicole. If someone came to you with a baby and said it was yours— and then you learned that it was really your brother's child—could you simply put it out of your mind and walk away?"

"*I* couldn't," Nicole said slowly. "But I'm having a hard time figuring out why *you* can't. You're not exactly noted for your ability to make commitments, you know. The article I read about you said that you refuse to make plans more than a few days in advance to avoid feeling trapped. That you won't write with a pen, only a pencil, because ink is too permanent."

Drake stiffened. "The writer of that article is guilty of character assassination and is one of the many reasons why I refuse to do interviews anymore. Anyway, none of that crap has anything to do with my brother's child."

"Well, anyone who feels trapped by ink ought to run—not walk—away from a baby. Babies make demands that have to be met, day in and day out. Babies mean involvement. They're a total commitment."

"If you're trying to scare me by saying the C word, it's not working, Nicole," Drake said, mocking. "Do you want me to carry Robbie to the car?"

"You're as tenacious as gum stuck to the sole of a shoe," Nicole said crossly. "All right, you may drive us home, but I'll carry Robbie to the car. And once you've seen where we live, you're leaving."

"You do wonders for a man's ego, Nicole."

"Mister, your ego doesn't need any boosts. It's already as big as the World Trade Center."

Drake shot her an irritated look. She annoyed him. And yet—she amused him too. He'd never met anyone as outspoken as she. He was used to dealing with women who were too sophisticated to be frank. And too calculating. Every woman he met these days knew that he was a highly paid, well-connected success in the world of commercial and fashion photography. An "in" with him meant the possibility of lucrative exposure in magazine ads, covers, and stories.

There wasn't a model—aspiring or established—in all of New York who would glower at him while comparing him to a wad of gum on the bottom of a shoe! He'd become accustomed to being admired, acclaimed, and flattered by women. Nicole's reaction to him was unique. *She* was unique. And every single one of his well-honed self-protective instincts kicked in to deny the attraction she held for him.

He led the way to his sleek little Maserati Spyder, a sporty black two-door convertible. Nicole stared dubiously at the car. "I'm taking Robbie on the bus. This car isn't designed for a child's safety. It would be criminal negligence to put a baby in an open convertible."

He reluctantly conceded that she might have a point, though a bit overstated. "I'll put the top on."

Nicole considered it, then shook her head. "The

bus is air-conditioned. On a hot day like today, it'll be more comfortable to—"

"I can't believe that any sane person would prefer the Newark city bus system to my new car!" He sounded mortally aggrieved. "But it just so happens that I have air-conditioning installed in this car. Does that suit milady?"

"Air-conditioning in a convertible?" Nicole arched her brows. "You really do have money to burn, don't you?"

He knew she didn't mean it as a compliment. Drake was flummoxed. He was used to women rhapsodizing over his exotic, expensive cars. Nicole fretted all through Newark about the lack of a child safety seat and the dangers of the soft, convertible roof which he'd dutifully put in position.

Nor was she at all interested in hearing about his three other cars—the eye-popping indigo Porsche Cabriolet, the elegant white Bitter SC convertible, and the unforgettable fire-engine-red Ferrari Testarossa which he kept at his home in East Hampton. "Four cars is a trifle short of a zillion," he added a bit defensively, thinking of that irksome article she'd read. He decided not to mention his three boats.

"Four cars and they're all overpriced and impractical. Four cars and each one seats only two people. How stupid," Nicole said succinctly. "My idea of a real dream car is a big wood-paneled station wagon or one of those wonderful Dodge Caravans. You can put whole families in them."

"You know, I have an inkling as to how the group leaders in your NOW chapter felt when they asked you to leave," Drake said with forced levity. "It was either that or throttle you. You're a real grind, Nicole. Dodge Caravans and day care are so prosaic. What's wrong with some flash? Some glamour? What do you have against hot cars and female CEO's, anyway?"

"Nothing, as long as the practical priorities are

met first. But the majority of women are more concerned with their children's welfare than whether or not a woman is CEO of AT and T. So lets direct our time and energy to affordable, quality day care first and then—"

"You sound like a tape-recorded sermon. Help! How do I turn you off?"

"You've been amazingly successful in turning me off."

"What's this? Earnest, forthright Ms. Fortune indulging in a double-entendre?" He cast her a sly glance as they idled at a traffic light. "And one based on a totally false premise, too. I turn you on, Nicole. We both know it."

A wave of heat rippled through her. She concentrated on adjusting the straps of Robbie's colorful sunsuit. "Please spare me the slick, sexual banter, Drake. It sounds as canned to me as my day care spiel does to you."

He felt as if he'd been doused with a bucket of icy water. True, it might've sounded like a rendition of the slick, sexual banter that was his stock-in-trade, but only he knew that it had been something more. He'd been seeking an admission from her. He wanted her to acknowledge that he aroused her.

His lips thinned to a tight, straight line. And what would he have done if she had? Admit that she excited him in a way that he couldn't explain, that he couldn't understand? He had to remember whom he was dealing with, he reminded himself. Nicole Fortune was an unknown element, possibly a destructive element, and he had to be on his guard with her.

Nicole was more than willing to let the sexually charged moment pass. "Turn left here," she directed.

They drove in silence through several long blocks of run-down tenements, vacant lots, and abandoned buildings. The oppressive heat had driven scores of people out of their stifling homes. Groups of youths congregated on the street corners, older people sat on cement stoops or stairs, children played on the sidewalks.

"I think the difference in temperature between inside the car and out on the streets is at least thirty degrees," Nicole remarked. "I almost need a blanket for Robbie in here."

"Now I fully understand the phrase 'to damn with faint praise,' " Drake said drolly.

"I don't mean to sound like a whining nag, Drake. It's very kind of you to give us a ride. Faster than the bus, and cooler too," she admitted with a distinctly mischievous grin.

He was thrown totally off balance by her smile and sudden shift in mood. He decided that he liked it better when she was arguing with him. Then, he didn't have to contend with the surge of desire which made his body tighten. He didn't have to restrain himself from wanting to take her hand and lay it on his thigh, interlacing his fingers with hers.

She directed him onto a side street lined with narrow houses in various states of disrepair. "Right there, that's my house," she said, pointing to an aging three-story brick row house surrounded by a dilapidated fence.

"Pull right in front of the house," she suggested, her eyes flicking over the luxurious black interior of the small car. "Around here, the term 'hot car' has a completely different meaning."

"I can imagine." Drake glanced up and down the block. Nicole and baby Robbie lived here? He wasn't at all pleased with what he saw.

Nicole correctly interpreted the disapproval shadowing his face. "The neighborhood has—uh—deteriorated somewhat during the past few years. It used to be nice."

"During your lifetime?" Drake asked doubtfully. "Nicole, calling this place a deteriorating neighborhood is too high a compliment. This whole area is a slum."

She couldn't argue with him there. Nicole shrugged. "At least I own the house free and clear. Mom and I made the final mortgage payment before she left the country three years ago."

Drake gazed at the house. Owning it seemed more of a nightmare than a reason for satisfaction. He thought of his own sprawling, meticulously maintained property in exclusive East Hampton. The contrast between there and here was almost too vast to comprehend.

Nicole opened the car door and gathered the sleeping baby close. "Thanks for the ride, Drake," she called breezily, climbing out. "Have a nice trip back to New York."

"Wait a minute, I'm not going back yet. We haven't talked. We—"

Nicole groaned. "We have talked and you are going back." She hurried to unlatch the rusty front gate. "Good-bye."

Drake got out of the car and started to follow her. "Nicole, I'm coming inside with you."

"You can't. Your car won't last ten minutes out here unattended. No, make that five. I'm sure the word is already spreading about this car. The moment you're out of sight, it'll be gone."

Drake was appalled. He glanced around him and could almost feel dozens of pairs of unseen eyes leering at his defenseless little car. He watched Nicole scurry up the chipped cement walk to the front door of the house, then stared at his car, feeling truly torn.

It was hot and stuffy inside the house and the few fans circulating the air did little to alleviate the heat. Nicole carried Robbie to the second-floor bedroom he shared with her and laid him in his crib. He didn't awaken, but rolled onto his stomach and tucked his plump little legs under him. She stroked his soft, spiky hair. He was already beginning to perspire from the warmth of the room.

Nicole gazed at him, her heart swelling with love. There was nothing she wouldn't do to keep him safe and happy, she silently promised.

Did that include keeping him from his paternal relatives and an inheritance that would guarantee him a home and a life far more luxurious than she could ever hope to give him? taunted the contentious devil's advocate who lived inside her head. Nicole sighed.

Why did she have to internally debate everything? It was difficult enough taking on the world at large without continually arguing with herself too. Lost in thought, she nearly collided with Peter, her foster brother, who was coming down the hall with an enormous Great Dane trotting at his side.

"It's awfully quiet around here," she observed, smiling at Peter. "Where are Hailey and the kids?"

Peter, blond, blue-eyed, and slight, considered the question for several long moments. "They went to the store to get Popsicles," he said at last.

"Have you fed Demon?" She patted the dog's huge head and he drooled happily. "Did you have your lunch yet, Peter?"

Peter looked confused. "I don't know."

"Why don't we go to the kitchen and decide?" Nicole tried to take Peter's hand but he drew it away and thrust it deep into his pocket. "I'm sorry, Peter. Some days you don't mind being touched." And some days he couldn't tolerate it. She knew from long experience that it was impossible to predict how much contact he could accept on any given day.

Suddenly Demon gave a ferocious bark and bounded down the stairway to leap at the front door. Nicole charged after him. "Be quiet, Demon! If you wake up Robbie, I'll—"

"He's just doing his job, Nicole," Peter admonished, following her. "He's guarding our house from that guy out front who just paid Remondo to be his lookout."

Nicole stared at him. Sometimes Peter was completely in touch with his surroundings and totally alert and aware of everything going on around him. Other times, he was in his own world where only he saw and heard things. It fell to her to interpret which world he was currently residing in.

"Were you looking out the window, Peter? Did you see a man give Remondo some money?"

Peter nodded. "And he's coming up to our door. He must think this is the crack house."

The doorbell rang at that moment and the dog went wild, jumping at the door in a barking frenzy. Nicole's eyes widened in alarm. "Go away," she called through the closed door. "If you don't leave now, we'll turn the dog loose. He's trained to kill."

"Nicole?" Drake's voice sounded through the heavy door. "What's going on in there?"

"It's Drake!" Nicole said with a gasp. Relief flowed through her. "It's okay, Peter. Open the door." She restrained the dog by holding his collar as Peter flung open the door.

"Demon isn't really a killer," Peter announced to a bewildered-looking Drake. "We just say that to scare people. We thought you wanted the crack house and came here by mistake." He stared out the door at the car and the muscular giant standing beside it. "You gave Remondo some money."

"Remondo?" Drake followed his line of vision. "You mean the Incredible Hulk out there? Yeah, I gave him fifty bucks to watch my car."

"I'm going out to watch Remondo watch the car, Nicole," Peter announced solemnly.

"Okay, but take Demon with you." Nicole snapped a leash onto the dog's collar and turned him over to Peter.

"I haven't been this confused since I saw my

first Fellini film," Drake said, watching Peter walk stiffly with the dog toward his car and the behemoth guarding it. He turned back to Nicole. "Now I feel like I've wandered into one. Who's the spaced-out zombie with the horse on a leash?"

The change in Nicole was vivid and startling. Her body tensed and sparks seemed to shoot from her eyes. "Don't you dare make fun of Peter!" Her voice was a low, distinctly threatening growl. Drake stared at her in surprise. She not only sounded menacing, she somehow managed to look menacing as well.

"Very impressive," he drawled. "I didn't take it seriously when you said those poor suckers who tangled with you lived to regret it. Now I'm beginning to believe it."

"Peter is my foster brother," Nicole said coldly. "And he's not a spaced-out zombie. If your glib little quip about him was supposed to be entertaining, it badly missed its mark."

Twin spots of color stained Drake's cheeks. "I'm sorry," he said quietly. He felt both foolish and ashamed, something he'd hadn't experienced in a long, long time.

"Those glib little quips roll quite easily off my tongue. It's become known as my style." He didn't bother to add that everyone he knew seemed to enjoy it. He could guess what Nicole's reply would be to that. "I didn't mean to offend you or your foster brother." His brow narrowed thoughtfully. "Does he live here with you too?"

Nicole nodded. "Peter came to live with us when he was twelve and has been with us on and off ever since. He's twenty-six now—and—and he's doing quite well."

"On and off meaning between hospitalizations?" Drake guessed shrewdly. "*Psychiatric* hospitalizations? And he lives here in the same house as you and little Robbie?"

"Peter has been diagnosed as schizophrenic, although I don't believe in labeling people." Nicole scowled. "And if you're going to imply that living with Peter is some kind of a risk, don't bother. Because it's not."

"It's not? Nicole, the papers are full of stories of psychos going beserk and—"

"Peter isn't a psycho! And he's not violent, he never has been. When I lose my temper—which I'm about to do with you—*I'm* infinitely more dangerous than he could ever be."

Drake tried to summon the apathy and aloofness which had always sustained him. It didn't work. What was happening to him? he wondered as he began to pace back and forth. He felt frustrated, angry, and involved—and he hated the feeling! But he simply couldn't detach himself from this situation, as he had from so many others in the past.

"It's not right, Nicole!" he railed. "Robbie's grandfather is Preston Austin, a millionaire many times over. Robbie's father left a sizable estate as well. Yet you and the baby are living in a slum in a house with a—a deranged mental case and—"

Nicole's reaction was reflexive, conditioned by years of defending her foster sisters and brothers from the hurt and ridicule the outside world seemed to inflict so easily upon them. She let him have it right in the solar plexus with an expertly placed fist.

Drake gasped for breath and doubled over, clutching his middle. For a few moments, he considered falling to the floor and writhing in agony. He might have done just that if Nicole hadn't linked her arm around his waist and guided him to a well-worn sofa in the darkened living room. He leaned heavily against her.

"Oh, Drake, I'm sorry." Nicole observed his ashen face with alarm. "Come and sit down." He sank down onto the sofa and she hovered above him. "I shouldn't have hit you," she said regretfully. "It's been years since I've hit anyone."

"Well, you haven't lost your touch," Drake murmured on a groan. "God, you really socked me, Nicole. I should hit you back, except I was raised not to hit women. Anyway, I'm too winded to even try."

"I'm terribly sorry," Nicole said, her blue eyes filled with remorse. "I didn't think, I just reacted." That was the epitaph they were going to engrave on her tombstone if she didn't mend her ways, she thought glumly.

She drew a sharp, shaky breath. "You see, for years I had to protect the kids who lived here with Mom and me from all the bullies in the neighborhood and at school. The only way to do it was to be meaner and tougher than they were. Most times that meant acting first and thinking later."

Drake continued to breathe in short, shallow gasps. "Did you ever consider a career in the ring? I think you'd give Tyson or Holmes a run for their money."

"The punch I threw is the only one I know," Nicole confessed. "I mostly relied on kicking, biting, gouging, and scratching. I was a dirty rotten fighter . . . but I never had to fight anyone more than once. After I was through with them, they were careful not to harass poor little Peter and the others."

Drake leaned back against the sofa cushions and closed his eyes. The thousands of jangling nerve endings that had taken the brunt of her assault were slowly beginning to calm. The sharp, shooting pains lessened and breathing became easier.

Nicole watched him with concern. "I did try to warn you that I was far more dangerous than Peter could ever be. He's never attacked anyone in his life. He retreats into his own world and sort of drifts away."

"Yeah, well, you sure proved your point, lady. I think I'd rather face old Remondo armed with a Uzi than rile your temper again."

Now that he was recovering, a groundswell of pure male rage poured through him. She'd flattened him, yet because she was a woman he wasn't supposed to retaliate. But she sure didn't fight like any woman he'd ever known, he conceded. And even though he was furious and humiliated, part of him actually admired her. Not only did she protect her own, she was damn good at it.

It occurred to him that baby Robbie was lucky to have her for a mom. He thought of his own mother during his growing up years. She'd been gentle, dependent, and fearful. Weak. Unable to shield herself and her son from the cruel remarks and actions of a hostile town. His lips curved into a slight smile. Both his mother and the child he had been could've used an avenging champion like Nicole Fortune back in those bleak days.

"Are you feeling better?" Nicole hovered solicitously over him. She dared to touch his forehead which was clammy with perspiration. "I'll get you a cold drink. What would you like? Water, iced tea, or Kool-Aid?"

"How about a triple shot of Jack Daniels on the rocks?"

She cast him a speaking glance and left the room, returning a couple of minutes later with two tall glasses of iced tea. She handed him one and sat down beside him with the other. They both sipped their drinks in a silence broken only by the whirring of the fan on a nearby table.

Drake was the first to speak. "Your . . . brother said something about a crack house. Was he . . . uh . . . er . . . being delusional?"

Nicole shook her head. "Reality around here is more bizarre than any of Peter's hallucinations. A crack house opened down the block two months ago." She set her empty glass on the table and stared grimly into space. "This neighborhood has never been the best but since that place opened . . ." Her voice dropped. "It's becoming intolerable. I've talked to the neighbors—we all hate what's happening here. Anybody who can is getting out."

"Which is exactly what you should do, Nicole."

"And go where? First I'd have to sell the house and as you might've guessed, it's not exactly a seller's market around here. I don't think I could find a buyer. So where would we live? There's Peter, Hailey and the kids, Robbie, me, and the dog. We wouldn't all fit into a small apartment, which is all I could afford without money from the sale of the house."

For some reason, knowing that she'd thought about leaving depressed him. It would've been easier to shrug and turn away if she'd told him that this was paradise, she loved living here and never wanted to move. But she wanted to go and couldn't.

He swallowed the last of his iced tea and set the glass aside. He felt as if he were suffocating in this room. The curtains were drawn and the windows closed and locked, to keep out sun and burglars respectively.

"How do you stand it?" he blurted out. "All those people dependent on you? You're trapped here! Literally!"

"At least I'm living with people I love and who love me," Nicole retorted. "You're all alone. You have a big house in the country and an apartment in the city and all those cars and no one to share them with. *I* feel sorry for *you*."

Drake was incensed. "Well, don't waste your sympathy on me, sweetie. My life suits me perfectly. I live alone because I like it . . . and whenever I feel the urge for company, I have a Rolodex of names I can call. All I have to do is to extend the invitation and whoever I want to see arrives within the hour."

"What does that prove? The fact remains that you're not living with anyone you love—or who loves you."

"That's exactly the way I want it!" he roared. "You've got a helluva nerve implying otherwise."

"Hmm, so Mr. Mellow and Laid-back isn't so mellow and laid-back when it comes to talking about his lonely life?" Nicole surveyed him archly.

"Lonely life?" Drake howled. He was practically apoplectic at the very idea. "Baby, my life is the stuff other men's fantasies are made of!"

"I think you've gone from poor little poor boy to poor little rich boy. But you're still not happy, are you, Drake?"

"I'm happy, dammit!" He jumped to his feet. "I've succeeded beyond my wildest dreams. I have everything I've ever wanted."

"No, you don't." Nicole stood up too. "You don't have a happy marriage and you don't have children. And more than anything in the world, you want to be part of a normal all-American family— the one you didn't have as a kid."

"Ha! Oh, that's funny, Nicole. *Really* funny!"

"If I'm such a comedienne, then why aren't you laughing?" She proceeded to answer her own question. "Because I nailed it, didn't I? You want a family but you're too scared to give marriage a try. Because you value it so much, you're terrified that you might fail and—"

"I'm not listening to another second of your pretentious armchair psychology, *Dr. Freud*! Not only are you a feminist reject, you're also a washout at psychoanalysis!" Drake stalked furiously from the room. Before he had taken more than a few steps he was back, circling her like an angry lion. "The same theory could be applied to you too, you know. You were just as much a bastard as I was, on the outside looking in at all the cozy little families."

"I know," Nicole said calmly. "That's why I understand you so well."

"Oh, do you?" For some inexplicable reason, her matter-of-fact response enraged him. How dare she understand him! How dare she shake him from the comfortable complacency he'd worked so hard to achieve!

"Sorry to disappoint you, baby, but you don't understand me at all. If you did, you'd know better than to accuse me—"

"I didn't accuse you of anything. I simply stated—"

"Or to interrupt me when—"

"You interrupt me too," she reminded him. "In fact, you just did it again."

"You never know when to stop, do you, Nicole?" He stopped circling and stood stock still in front of her. "You push and push until I'm ready to—" He gripped her arms and yanked her against him. "Until I have to—"

Before Nicole had time to think or move or even breathe, his mouth was covering hers in a hard kiss. She reacted violently, struggling against him, but this time Drake had the element of surprise in his favor. He wrapped his arms tightly around her, pinning her arms between them, thus rendering them useless.

She tried to pull her head free, but he wouldn't let her, keeping her neck angled and her mouth trapped beneath his own. She tried to buck him with her body, but each movement brought forth a stunning awareness of her breasts pillowed against the hardness of his chest, of the burgeoning heat of his thighs against her own supple limbs.

And then, suddenly, she stopped fighting. It wasn't a conscious decision, but a purely instinctive one. She stopped thinking and her emotions promptly took over, responding on their own to the chemistry arcing between them. With a soft whimper of surrender, she relaxed against him, slowly, tentatively slipping her arms around his neck.

She parted her lips for the bold, insistent thrust of his tongue, and he kissed her deeply, possessively, his hands moving boldly over her soft curves. Her breasts swelled and pressed sensuously against the hardness of his chest and she began to rotate her hips unconsciously in an erotic feminine motion. She felt the driving force of his masculinity grind against her and she grew moist with need. All sense of time and place was obliterated by the stark hunger raging through her.

Nicole writhed in his arms, trying to get closer. She couldn't get enough of him. For the first time in her life, she experienced the primitive, deeply feminine need to envelop a man, to absorb him into her very being.

Their mouths were hot and hungry and their kiss grew deeper and longer and wilder. Drake filled her mouth with his tongue, probing hotly, and she moaned as a tide of passion stormed over her. Her hands moved greedily over the hard strength of his shoulders and back, caressing him.

Groaning deep in his throat, Drake cupped the soft fullness of her breasts in his hands, kneading sensuously. Her nipples were taut and pronounced against the fabric of her dress and he slowly, deftly, flicked his thumbs over them, back and forth, up and down, until she was moaning and twisting with need.

His mouth never leaving hers, his hands caressing her breasts, Drake deftly inched her over to the sofa. They were just a step away from sinking down onto the cushions when a loud clattering on the porch, followed by the ringing of the doorbell, sent shock waves crashing over them.

Abruptly, they broke apart. Nicole gazed at Drake, feeling strangely disoriented. She was breathless and trembling—and stunned by her incendiary response to him. He had taken her into his arms and she'd dissolved into a wild thing, governed by the intensity of her emotions. She felt a shiver of anxiety ripple through her. No one had ever had such power over her. And the realization that Drake Austin, of all people, should be the one to possess it, was totally unnerving.

Drake stared back at her, equally dazed. He'd touched her and lost all control, all sense of propriety. His blue eyes shifted from her face to the soft roundedness of her breasts. He wanted to see them, to cup them in his hands, to taste them. . . . His blood pulsed hotly and heavily, making him grow harder and tighter with every heartbeat.

Compulsively, Nicole followed his gaze, feeling his eyes upon her. It was as though he were physically touching her. She felt a soft thrust of sensation in her nipples and sharp little spears of excitement pierced the hot, secret core of her.

Neither were capable of speech. A taut sexual tension pulsated between them. Drake felt wired, his whole body an aching force of desire and need. He couldn't remember the last time a woman had turned him on so fast and so hard. And the realization that Nicole Fortune, of all people, should be the one to do it, was unnerving in the extreme.

The doorbell rang again and again. Nicole fought her way out of the thick sensual languor engulfing her. "That's probably Peter. I must've locked the door. I do it from sheer force of habit." She was aware that she was chattering nervously to fill the silence between them.

Dragging her eyes away from him, she hurried to the front door and opened it. A petite young woman with thick, dark hair framing her delicate, elfin face, herded three dark-haired, dark-eyed moppets into the house. "Nicole, did you know that Peter—" she began breathlessly.

"Well, well, well. This must be sister Hailey and the kiddies."

Both Nicole and Hailey whirled around at the sound of the husky masculine voice. Drake ambled into the hallway and lounged casually against the door frame. "I'm Drake Austin," he drawled.

"Robbie's father?" squeaked Hailey.

"Robbie's uncle," corrected Drake. "His father was my half brother Andrew. My late half brother. I'm sure Nicole will fill you in on all the details." His eyes flickered over the children. "What were they eating that turned them orange?"

"Popsicles," cried the oldest child, a little boy of four.

Appearing somewhat confused, Hailey turned her big, dark eyes back to Nicole. "Nicole, do you think it's a good idea for Peter and Demon to go for a ride in Remondo's new car? I tried to tell him that he ought to clear it with you first but—"

"Remondo's new car?" Nicole and Drake chorused together.

They both ran out of the house in time to see Remondo, in the driver's seat, pull the sporty little Maserati Spyder away from the curb. The top had been removed and Peter sat in the passenger seat, his face devoid of expression. Demon was sitting proudly in the tiny backseat, his tongue hanging out of his mouth. He gave an enthusiastic bark as the car sped into the street.

Four

"Come back here!" shouted Drake and began to run down the street after the car. The racy little Maserati Spyder picked up speed, leaving its owner far, far behind. It was out of sight before Drake reached the end of the block.

His strenuous burst of exertion in the steamy city heat left him drenched in perspiration, and he trudged back to the house where Nicole stood waiting for him on the sidewalk. Hailey and the three children had joined her there.

"That sonofabitch stole my car!" Drake was outraged. "I paid him fifty bucks to watch it for a few minutes and he stole it!"

"I'm sure it's not stolen," Nicole said in a placating tone which doubly increased his ire.

"He hot-wired it and drove off in it! That sure as hell smacks of car theft to me! Where's your phone? I'm going to call the police and report—"

"You can't report it to the police," Nicole countered. Her calm was immediately replaced by an urgent intensity. "They'll pick up Remondo and charge him with grand larceny. He'll go to jail."

"Sounds good to me!" snapped Drake.

"No." Nicole shook her head. "Remondo isn't a

bad kid. Besides, Peter is with him. If they arrest Remondo, they'll charge Peter too."

Drake scowled. "As well they should. He's an accessory."

Hailey clasped her hands to her mouth in horror. "Peter can't go to jail! Nicole, do something!"

"Peter isn't going to jail," Nicole assured her, "and neither is Remondo." She turned her intense blue eyes on Drake. "Remondo is much younger than Peter but he's always been kind to him, he's always looked out for him. He'd never involve Peter in a crime, I'm sure of that. They've just gone for a little ride, that's all. They'll be back."

"Is that supposed to be reassuring?" Drake growled. "Do you really expect me to ignore the fact that a hoodlum, a schizo, and a dog are joyriding around Newark in my brand-new car?"

Hailey began to cry. "Oh, this is awful! Please, Mr. Austin, don't press charges! You have every right to be furious, but—"

"He's not going to press charges, Hailey," Nicole interrupted. She addressed her foster sister, but her eyes were fixed on Drake.

Once again he was struck by their piercing blue color and the quiet, confident power reflected within them. Nicole Fortune was accustomed to making things turn out her way. He recognized that implacable determination in her because he possessed it himself. At any other time he probably would've admired her for it. But now . . .

"I've only had that car for five days, Nicole! It was completely customized and—"

"It's still only a car," Nicole cut in. "Remondo and Peter are *people* and worth far more consideration than a stupid little sports car."

"If you don't stop referring to my cars as stupid, I won't be responsible for my actions, Nicole."

"All right," she conceded with a grace that surprised him. "It's not a stupid car." She raised her eyes to his. "It's become a bad habit of mine, calling things that don't matter to me stupid. I do it too often, I know. I'm sorry, Drake."

Her candor disarmed him, and so did her unexpected apology. She possessed a superb sense of timing, he thought wryly. Just when he was ready to wring her neck, she would say something which turned the situation completely around in her favor. Living in a world of prima donnas with their accompanying world-class egos, he wasn't accustomed to anyone acknowledging faults or mistakes. He seldom did so himself! Though he tried to hang onto his righteous fury and indignation, he was aware that Nicole had successfully defused it.

"But even though your car isn't stupid, it still isn't as important as Peter and Remondo," Nicole added gravely. "If you press charges, Remondo will have a felony on his record and his mother will be heartbroken." She set her jaw and tilted her chin, her blue eyes fierce. "And if you think I'll let anyone put my poor little brother in jail, you're grossly mistaken."

"How can Peter be your *little* brother when he's two years older than you are?" Drake's tone was decidedly testy, but resigned as well. As much as it galled him, he knew he wasn't going to call the police and report his car stolen. Yet.

"He's shorter than I am, that makes him my little brother," Nicole retorted, but her eyes were gleaming. She'd won a reprieve for Remondo and Peter and she knew it. "Thanks for understanding, Drake. I know they'll bring the car back shortly."

She turned on the full force of her smile and its effects sent him reeling. Her smile was genuine, full of inviting warmth and humor and sensuality. It dazzled him; it made him want to please her, to accede to her every wish so she would smile that way at him again.

Drake drew in a deep, steadying breath. *Maybe*

you should sign over the title of the car to Remondo and Peter? a snide little voice inside his head taunted him. That would certainly please Miss Fortune. Why, she might even treat him to another one of those head-spinning smiles.

He took a few wary steps back, fighting to recover his senses. That smile of hers was a dangerous weapon when it could turn a cool, self-possessed man like himself into a panting, eager puppy dog!

"I'm going to take the children inside and clean them up," Hailey said nervously, her eyes flicking from Drake to Nicole. "It's so hot today, they'll enjoy a long, cool bath."

"I'm sure they will." Nicole smiled at her and the children. "We'll wait out here for Peter and Remondo to come back."

"*If* they ever come back," muttered Drake. "*If* they aren't halfway to the Canadian border by now."

Nicole's lips twitched and she tried and failed to suppress a smile. "We have an extradition treaty with Canada, don't we? *If* they were to enter Canada in a stolen car, I'm sure the police would be delighted to return them. Along with the car, of course."

"You're patronizing me!"

"Maybe." She smiled again. "Just a little. You deserve it."

Once again her honesty floored him. He fought the urge to smile back. She could charm him without even trying and the realization unnerved him. In pure self-defense, he attempted to work himself back into another indignant rage. "My car is stolen by your brother and his delinquent cohort and *you* have the nerve to adopt an insufferably condescending air toward *me*?"

Someone less impulsively outspoken might've tried to soothe his ruffled masculine ego. Being Nicole, she did not. "Meaning you're the only one who should be permitted to adopt an insufferably condescending air?" She'd never been one to pander to egos, ruffled, masculine, or otherwise.

"Why should that be? Because you're the sensational, sought-after, successful Drake Austin?" She eyed him archly. "Careful, Drake, you're in danger of believing your own press clippings. Always a hazardous side effect of fame, I'm told."

He stared at her in astonishment. "You're really good at this, you know? I've never met anyone as adept at turning the tables as you are. You're a regular pro! For all practical purposes, you should be crying and begging me to have mercy on your brother who's gotten himself involved in a felony by stealing my car! Hailey had the right idea. But you—*you* end up lecturing me on the evils of fame. What do you want from me, lady? An apology for minding that my car was stolen?"

His words gave her pause. "You're right, I'm very good at fighting back," she agreed thoughtfully. "Not only physically, but verbally. I've had to be. I learned a long, long time ago that crying and begging get you nowhere."

"Well, that's the truth." Drake nodded. He marveled at her ability to divert him, even as he allowed himself to be diverted. "I learned that, too. Only the strong survive, as the saying goes."

"But the strong ones have a responsibility to the weak. You believe that, too," she added when he rolled his eyes and laughed derisively.

"You were right the first time, honey. It's a tough world and not everybody makes it. The strong trample the weak. That's just the way it is."

"If that's the way it is, then what are you doing here in Newark, Drake? Why are you determined to see Robbie receive his share of your brother Andrew's estate? He's a helpless baby—you can't get much weaker than that. And the Austins are rich and powerful and strong. So why aren't you trampling all over his rights to inherit his father's money?"

Drake scowled. "Robbie may be a helpless baby, but with *you* for a mother, he's hardly weak. I'm beginning to think you could hold your own against my father any day of the week."

"Unlike your mother," Nicole said shrewdly and watched the color slowly suffuse his face. "I'm right, aren't I? You remember what it was like for you as a child, living with a woman who was one of the weak, who couldn't stand up for herself or her son. You and your mother got trampled by the strong, all right. And now you think it's happening all over again with Robbie, and you want to prevent it."

Drake was alarmed at her perception. She comprehended entirely too much. She seemed to see right through him and that alarmed him even more. How could he maintain the cool, mellow, and laid-back image he'd so carefully cultivated with *her* around? How could he remain indifferent and detached when she infuriated him, challenged him, turned him on, and intrigued him as no one before ever had?

And she'd been Andrew's lover. She'd given birth to Andrew's son. The sharp, searing sensation which ripped through him at the thought was physical in its intensity. He'd always known how much Andrew hated him, how much Andrew had resented the very existence of an older, illegitimate half brother. As far as Andrew Austin was concerned, the fact that Drake had been taller, stronger, a better athlete, brighter, and more popular during their growing-up years had added intolerable insult to his sense of injury. Drake's phenomenally successful career in photography, which he'd achieved entirely on his own, had embittered the lazy, self-indulgent Andrew all the more.

Andrew and Nicole. The image of them together

burned itself into Drake's very soul. She seemed the antithesis of everything the spoiled, self-centered Andrew had been. But was she really what she seemed to be?

He gazed into her deep blue eyes, feeling confused and exposed and terribly vulnerable. He hadn't felt this way since he was very young. And only two other people had ever been able to engender such feelings in him: his father Preston and his brother Andrew, by their steadfast rejection. But that had been a long time ago, and years ago he'd developed a protective armor to shield himself. It had remained effective and in place until today, when Nicole Fortune had effortlessly pierced it.

He felt threatened and angry. He hated these feelings, and he wanted to be rid of them. How dare she evoke them? He wanted to be rid of her, too. He wanted to get out of Newark and never look back.

Except he was stuck here because her crazy brother and his felonious friend had stolen his car! Agitatedly, Drake began to pace back and forth on the sidewalk in front of the house.

Nicole watched him for a few minutes. "You're going to get heat stroke," she warned. "Let's go into the house and have another glass of iced tea."

"So you can continue your little seduction?" Drake's pale blue eyes flicked over her with deliberately insulting dismissal. "No thanks, baby."

Nicole's cheeks flushed scarlet. She was out of her league with him when it came to sexual gibes and she knew it.

"Going to let that one pass?" Drake taunted. He was determined to distance her from himself; he'd inadvertently let her come way too close. "Why, Nicole? You're so good with words. Are you equally talented in bed, I wonder?"

"You'll never know!" She thought of all those

beautiful women he had photographed, all those nude, perfect bodies he had seen. And taken to bed as well? She thought of the passionate kiss they'd shared and felt an internal liquid heat that surpassed the blazing temperatures outside. And then she looked at Drake, who was watching her with those mocking eyes of his, who had just accused her of trying to seduce him and then rejected her with a cool "no thanks."

He obviously didn't share her shattering memory of their kiss. Nicole's heart clenched. How could she have been naive enough to think that he had been as passionately aroused, as deeply affected by their kiss as she had been? The man was a wordly sexual sophisticate, she reminded herself. Such a kiss must be as commonplace for him as it was rare for her.

She felt foolish and hurt and hopelessly inexperienced. As competent and self-assured as she was in so many areas of her life, she knew she was woefully lacking when it came to sex. And she was well aware that a twenty-four-year-old virgin was considered an anomaly of the times. That was her, all right, she thought glumly. A twenty-four-year-old virgin anomaly.

Nicole swallowed. She didn't often feel vulnerable, but she felt that way now. Thanks to one Drake Austin. "I'm going inside to check on Robbie," she said tightly. "Since Hailey is busy with her kids in the tub, she won't be able to go to him if he's awake."

Drake said nothing and she turned and walked to the front door of the house without another word. He watched her, admiring her graceful stride, the subtle way her hips moved, the shapeliness of her legs. She disappeared inside without once casting a glance back at him, and he sucked in his breath and squinted against the relentless afternoon sun. Even when he donned his sunglasses, it was almost too bright to be bearable.

But he almost welcomed the discomfort for it distracted him from his unsettling feelings for Nicole.

When Nicole emerged from the house about twenty minutes later, holding a beaming Robbie in her arms, Drake was still standing in the sun on the sidewalk.

"Yes, I'm still here," he said caustically, fighting against responding to the appealing picture she and the baby made. "Still waiting for Remondo's innocent joyride to come to an end. How long do I have to wait before I'm allowed to call it a car theft, Nicole? And to report my car stolen?"

Robbie made a chortling sound and bounced up and down in Nicole's arms. "The kid thinks it's funny." Drake grimaced. "Even he can't believe I was stupid enough to watch my car get stolen and do nothing about it. The police will get a good laugh over it too, I'm sure." He raised his voice to a ridiculous falsetto. "I didn't think those nice boys were stealing my car, officer, I thought they were simply borrowing it for a while."

"I don't blame you for getting impatient," said Nicole. "I was sure they'd be back by now. I'm starting to get a little worried about them myself."

Forever after, Drake would be grateful that Remondo chose that moment to swing the sporty little car around the corner and into view, for he had absolutely no idea how to respond to her incredibly understated understatement. His immediate inclination was to laugh or to throttle her. The timely appearance of the Maserati Spyder fortunately precluded both courses of action.

"There they are!" Nicole cried, and pointed unnecessarily at the little black convertible heading toward them. "Oh look, Drake, Peter is smiling!"

Drake scowled. "Yeah, well, I'm not. And he sure as hell won't be smiling when I—"

"No, no, you don't understand," Nicole said, clutching at his arm. "You see, one of the most profound changes in Peter's personality since his

illness began has been his loss of pleasure. Anhe-
donia is the official word for it and it's one of the
saddest hallmarks of schizophrenia, although the
medical books hardly acknowledge it. You can't
imagine how terrible it's been to watch Peter's
humor and joy and affection just drain away. The
doctors say it's caused by some kind of imbalance
in his brain's biochemistry, but what it means is
that Peter seldom ever smiles or laughs. It's heart-
breaking, like watching the slow death of all his
spirit. To see him smiling like this—oh, Drake,
it's wonderful!"

Drake stared into her dark blue eyes which were
shimmering with tears, making them look as shiny
and bright as polished sapphires. He glanced down
at her fingers curved around his forearm. They
were slender and strong and he imagined them
touching him in passion, curving around the vi-
tal part of him which was already beginning to
swell with wanting. . . .

His mind clouded. Remondo's hair-raising swerve
onto the curb seemed almost irrelevant and anti-
climactic compared to the fantasies swirling in
his head.

Remondo braked the car to a halt and hopped
over the side. "Man, this car is baaad!"

Nicole's eyes were fixed on Peter who was still
smiling as he opened the door and slowly got out
of the car. Demon, occupying the tiny back seat,
barked in greeting and then jumped onto the
sidewalk.

"We had a good ride, Nicole," Peter said, looking
more animated than Drake previously had seen
him.

"We be cruisin' in style!" exclaimed Remondo.
He grabbed Peter's hand and took it through the
motions of an elaborate handshake, ending with
a fraternal, palm-to-palm slap. "Gotta go, dude,"
he called and raced down the street.

"Wait a minute!" Drake called, but Remondo

was already halfway down the block. He heaved an exasperated sigh and turned to Nicole. She gave him a beseeching look and shifted little Robbie in her arms.

Much against his will, he found himself melting, and it had nothing to do with the stifling urban heat. The sight of Nicole and the baby once again struck a deep chord within him. Add to that her big, blue eyes pleading with him to have mercy on her poor brother who'd lost his ability to laugh, yet was tentatively smiling now. . . .

Only Adolf Hitler could've resisted her, thought Drake. Resignedly, he turned to Peter and managed to produce a credible smile. "I'm glad you enjoyed the ride, Peter. You—er—like my car, eh?"

Peter nodded solemnly. "Remondo and I liked it. But Demon didn't."

Drake swung his gaze to the huge dog who was lying contentedly at Peter's feet. "Demon didn't like it?" he repeated carefully. He hoped Peter wasn't going to launch into some crazy delusional stuff. He really wasn't sure how to handle himself around a bona fide mental patient.

Peter shook his head. "He got carsick all over the back. Remondo said it was okay, though."

Drake hurried to the car and stared into the back in appalled silence. Peter wasn't hallucinating. Demon definitely had been sick.

"Peter, why don't you take Demon inside and give him a bowl of water?" Nicole suggested quickly. "It's so hot, I'm sure he's thirsty. Why don't you get yourself something to drink, too?"

Peter nodded. "That's a good idea." He gave the leash a gentle tug and the big dog scrambled to his feet.

Drake managed to maintain his silence until Peter and the dog were inside the house. And then: "Look at this mess!" he roared. "In a five-day-old car! And Remondo had the gall to say it's okay?"

Nicole stared at the defiled back seat. "It would've been nice if they'd cleaned it up," she murmured.

Drake glared at her. "You have a positive gift for stating the obvious, not to mention making inane understatements. If you're deliberately trying to infuriate me, honey, you've succeeded beyond your wildest dreams!"

"I'm trying not to make you any madder than you already are," retorted Nicole. "That's why I'm underplaying everything—to keep you from going into orbit."

"I never go into orbit!" snapped Drake. "I never even lose my temper!"

Nicole coughed discreetly.

"Today has been an unfortunate exception, Ms. Fortune. I'm normally cool and dispassionate. I possess enviable equanimity, but—"

"You have a lot of suppressed rage," Nicole injected. "You keep it well hidden under that laid-back facade of yours, but it's there. Why not channel it constructively, Drake? Use it to—"

"Commit mayhem?" His tone was chilling. "If I do, I'll start with you, and any jury in the world would acquit me. You and your—your clan have goaded me beyond human endurance and I—"

"I hate to interrupt your tirade, but I haven't had a chance to thank you for being so kind to Peter." She met his startled blue eyes with her own warm and earnest ones. "You were so gracious, Drake, you even smiled at him, and I know you didn't feel like smiling at the time. Peter can't handle it when people are angry and threatening with him—it's too stressful for him. Thank you so much for your understanding."

Drake held her gaze, blood roaring in his ears. She'd pricked his burst of anger as easily as a pin deflates a balloon. He continued to stare at her, feeling as stunningly off balance as he'd ever been.

Robbie made some cute baby noises and Nicole smiled down at him and replied with some sweetly maternal nonsense of her own. And in that moment Drake wanted her more than he'd ever wanted any woman in his life.

He felt thoroughly, helplessly ensnared by this fearfully insightful woman who'd given birth to Andrew's child, whose family was so very dependent upon her. She carried more complications than a dread disease, and he was suddenly terrified of being sucked in. It was an alarming possibility, he realized grimly. He felt too much for her too fast, and the unexpected depth and strength of his feelings evoked a sharp, internal panic. He had to get away from her, and fast.

"Don't try to ingratiate yourself with me, Nicole! It doesn't become you." He deliberately set the stage for another quarrel.

Nicole was quick to respond. The warmth abruptly left her eyes. He watched in fascination as they narrowed into glittering blue slits. "I've never been ingratiating in my entire life! You can't distinguish genuine appreciation from manipulative fawning, Drake Austin—and that says a lot about you and the shallow, self-indulgent life you lead!"

He felt adrenaline surge through his body, making him feel powerful and energetic and alive. It occurred to him that he liked fighting with her as much as he liked kissing her. And watching her. And wanting her. She was wrong when she accused him of not recognizing genuine appreciation. He did. He'd never been fooled by the fawning manipulations of those who catered to him to serve their own ends. Nicole was candid, honest, and straightforward. She would never kowtow to him.

The notion pleased him as much as it irked him. He wondered why. Maybe she was right, maybe his ego was comparable to the World Trade Center. *Was* he beginning to believe his own press? And then it struck him that this was Andrew's lover daring to lecture him on self-indulgence and egomania when Andrew had held the world's record in each of those categories. Nicole had been *Andrew's lover.* A primitive anger ripped through him. He couldn't contain it.

"Never been ingratiating? What a little hypocrite you are, Nicole. You were involved with Andrew, remember? And I knew my brother well enough to know that Andrew required fawning, flattery, and *ingratiation* from all his women. Hell, he demanded it from them!"

Nicole froze. The specter of Andrew Austin—and her own deception about Robbie—loomed again. Devious evasion and secrecy were not her strong suits. If Drake were around much longer, there was a very good chance that he'd learn the truth, because she'd end up blurting it out to him. She had to get him away from her. Now. She knew how to do it. She could be just as argumentative and insulting as he.

"It's definitely time for you to go back to New York and stop wasting my time," she ordered imperiously. "I'm tired of putting up with a—a jerk like you!"

"Jerk?" Drake was momentarily nonplussed. Jerks were cloddish misfits, barely tolerated by others. He'd never been that in his life. Even the negatives used to describe him—cool, aloof, fiercely ambitious—had a certain respectful ring to them. Even as a child, his peers had admired him. No one had ever called him a—"jerk?"

She nodded. "You do have your good points, but basically, you're a jerk, Drake Austin."

A jerk? He winced. Funny how such a mild taunt could have such a sting. Or was it because she was the one who was mocking him? Drake frowned. "I'm getting out of here. I've had all I can take from you."

How untrue that was! He wanted to take much, much more. He wanted to take *her*, her tempting mouth, her enticing curvaceous body. Worse, it didn't end there. As much as he wanted the hot physical possession, he wanted more from her, too. He wanted her strength and her humor and her indomitable spirit in his life as well.

Flashes of his commitment-free, unshackled, and liberated lifestyle tumbled through his mind and he contrasted it to the chaos and complexity that was Nicole's life. No, it was too much, he thought wildly. Even if she hadn't been Andrew's lover, her awesome sense of responsibility and everything it entailed made her all wrong for a cool, freewheeling guy like him.

Perspiring, his stomach tied in knots, Drake drew his money clip from his pocket and quickly peeled off two fifty-dollar bills. "Here, take this for the baby's first pair of shoes. This *jerk* is leaving—I won't waste any more of your valuable time."

Nicole immediately recoiled from the money. "I don't want anything from you!"

"Dammit, take it!" He grabbed her hand and thrust the cash in her palm, using his own fingers to close her fingers around the bills. He was close enough for Robbie to lean forward and grab his shirt with his eager little hands. Instinctively, Drake reached to lift the baby into his arms.

Robbie's sturdy, warm little body felt good to hold. He looked into the baby's big, coffee-brown eyes and felt a flash of recognition, an undeniable connection. Robbie had the same shape and color eyes as Andrew, Dane, and Ian Austin. Only Drake had inherited Preston Austin's blue eyes via Mendelian genetics and his blue-eyed mother.

Robbie grinned at him and made a grab for his nose. Drake chuckled and ducked his head. A surge of avuncular affection coursed through him. He wondered how and why he should feel a protective fondness for Andrew's child, while resenting Nicole for having been Andrew's lover.

Nicole watched Drake's face soften as he looked at Robbie. It was a touching, beautiful sight. She thought of the blood tie between them and her throat tightened. Was she wrong in coming between them?

She answered the question almost immediately. No, she wasn't. In her world, blood ties were irrelevant. Her family consisted of those who were in her life because they needed and loved her. Robbie certainly fit into that category. He was her child as surely as Peter and Hailey and Cheryl and all the rest were her brothers and sisters.

Drake's eyes met Nicole's over the top of Robbie's little head. Something intangible passed between them, but it was so real it took his breath away. It seemed impossible to believe that they'd just met today. He was powerfully affected by her. Her very presence evoked feelings so deep and aroused emotions so strong that they seemed joined by some primordial bond.

Nicole was experiencing the same breathtaking, psychic sensation. She'd never felt it before, and had no way of knowing that it was mutual. She was used to living in the cold world of reality, and such feelings seemed to exist strictly in the realm of romantic fantasy. *Stop daydreaming, Nicole,* she told herself sternly. Men like superstar Drake Austin weren't for the down-to-earth Nicole Fortunes of the world.

Robbie began to fuss, and his cries snapped them both to attention.

"I'd better take him inside," Nicole said quietly, her voice low and shaken from the intensity of their silent encounter. "The heat bothers him . . . he gets cranky when it's hot like this."

"I don't blame him." Drake handed the child to her. They were both careful to avoid each other's eyes. "Look, do you have any kind of room air-conditioner in there? It must be hell at night in those upstairs rooms."

"It's not that bad," Nicole lied. "It cools off at night some."

"Yeah, the temperature drops down into the eighties, I'll bet." Drake pulled out his billfold again and gave her the rest of the cash in it. "Buy an air conditioner for the baby's room, Nicole. If that's not enough, let me know."

Nicole stared at the fistful of dollars in her hand. She was nothing if not practical, and as thrilling as it might be to her pride, tossing the money in his face suddenly seemed like a stupid gesture. Especially when she'd been saving for months for an air conditioner for the hall which would, hopefully, cool off all the upstairs rooms.

"It's very generous of you," she said, staring at the ground. "Thank you, Drake."

Drake was studying the ground just as intently. "Well, I'd better go."

She nodded her agreement.

He stode to his car and drove off in a black blur of speed. Nicole watched him round the corner, and stood staring into the distance long after he'd disappeared from sight.

Five

The school term ended but the heat wave in Newark dragged on. A local water shortage prevented some of the city pools from being opened and even the temporary relief gained from opening an occasional fire hydrant was prohibited. Every day some unfortunate citizens, usually the very young or the very old, were hospitalized suffering from the ravages of the heat.

Thanks to Drake's donation, Nicole was able to buy a large portable air-conditioning unit which she installed in the hall window. It cooled the house considerably, although the individual rooms remained somewhat stuffy.

But no one in the Fortune household was complaining. Peter spent his days sitting in front of the air conditioner in the darkened hall with the ever loyal Demon at his side. Nicole and Hailey took care of the children and tried to keep them occupied and entertained, which required some ingenuity as not only the heat, but also the growing clientele for the neighborhood crack house, made venturing outside less and less desirable.

Not a single day went by that Nicole didn't think of Drake Austin, although it had been two weeks since the day they'd met—that fateful day when he'd kissed her, fought with her, and then left her. Not that she ever expected to hear from him again, she told herself bracingly, and launched into the severe scolding she administered to herself daily for mooning over him like an adolescent with a crush on an unobtainable rock or movie star. She'd never been one to get mired in hopelessness, and any possibility of herself and Drake Austin getting together definitely qualified as hopeless. She might just as well fancy herself taking up with Bruce Springsteen or Patrick Swayze!

The collect person-to-person call from Cheryl in California came in the middle of one weekday, the most expensive time to phone. And the most expensive way to call, too, of course. Nicole sighed as she accepted the charges. Cheryl wasn't one to consider economy.

Nor reality, as her breathless voice regaled Nicole with news of her latest love.

"Thad Griffin?" Nicole repeated incredulously, and Hailey, sitting at the kitchen table helping her children cut out doughy shapes, rolled her eyes heavenward. "Cheryl, you don't mean *the* Thad Griffin?"

"Yes! Yes, Nicole, I mean *him!*" Cheryl's breathy, little-girl voice chirped over the wire. "Oh, isn't it exciting, Nicole? I couldn't wait to tell you the news! I'm going to be in a movie!"

It was impossible to have picked up a newspaper or magazine during the last fifteen years without finding some mention of Thad Griffin, the handsome actor-turned-director whose reputation for award-winning films equaled his notoriety for numerous, tempestuous affairs.

Nicole groaned aloud. It seemed that Cheryl had stumbled into the arms of yet another Mr. Wrong. And furthermore: "Cheryl, didn't I just read in the paper that he's in big trouble with the IRS for some shady tax dealings? And with the immigration authorities, too, for hiring illegal aliens?"

"Oh, who cares?" Cheryl said blithely. "Nicole, he's so *cute!*"

Nicole clutched her head in her hands. "Cheryl, how did you happen to end up in California?" she asked, striving to remain calm. "The last time I heard from you, you were living in Miami selling jewelry in a boutique."

"That's where I met Thad!" exclaimed Cheryl. "The boutique was in this exclusive resort hotel and Thad came in one day and started talking to me. Oh, Nicole, it was love at first sight—just like in the movies! Thad said I would be perfect for this movie his company is going to make and brought me back to California with him. He won't be directing this one, his name isn't to be connected to the movie at all, but he expects to make a lot of money from it. And I'll make money too, Nicole! We start shooting tomorrow."

Nicole felt a foreboding chill. This didn't sound like one of Cheryl's hopeful fantasies with no basis whatsoever in reality. Instead, it had all the earmarks of one of the countless disasters Cheryl was forever becoming embroiled in. Like getting involved with Andrew Austin who'd made her pregnant to collect a cash prize.

Nicole took a deep, steadying breath. "Cheryl, you're sure this man really is Thad Griffin? He's not—er—someone pretending that he is?"

"He's really Thad, Nicole!" Cheryl giggled. "Do you think I wouldn't know that gorgeous face and fabulous body of his anywhere? Remember the poster of him I had in my room when I was in junior high?"

Nicole remembered. That was one suspicion ruled out. But her other doubt was even worse. "Cheryl, what kind of a movie is this going to be?" She gulped. "Honey, be honest with me. It isn't a—a porno movie, is it?"

"Oh, no, Nicole!" Cheryl sounded shocked. "Thad

loves me, he would never put me in a porno movie! This is an art film!"

Nicole stifled a groan. Cheryl in an art film? "Cheryl, I want you to promise me that if they tell you to take off your clothes or—or offer you any drugs, supposedly to 'relax you' while they film—I want you to leave right away and then call me. I'll send you a plane ticket home. Do you understand?"

"But, Nicole, I want to stay in California and be a movie star and marry Thad." Cheryl sounded thoroughly bewildered.

Nicole resisted the urge to scream. "Please, honey, listen to me. You know I only want you to be happy. Remember what I said and just say no."

"You sounded like Nancy Reagan," Hailey said dryly, when the phone call ended. "I wonder if she could get through to Cheryl?"

"Oh, Hailey, I have a bad feeling about this." Nicole sank into a chair. "Cheryl thinks Thad Griffin is going to marry her. God only knows what he's telling her—and what he intends to do with her. But I don't think that it has anything at all to do with marriage. Or art films."

"Cheryl is a genuine blond bombshell, Nicole," Hailey reminded her. "Men are always falling all over her. Maybe Thad Griffin really does want her."

"Oh, I have no doubt that he wants her for a lot of things, Hailey. But marriage isn't one of them. . . ."

Her voice trailed off. Thad Griffin wanting to marry Cheryl was about as unlikely as Drake Austin harboring a secret desire for Nicole Fortune, she thought grimly, and tried to ignore the depressing plummet of her heart.

Drake told himself that he ought to have Nicole's telephone number, strictly as a means of keeping tabs on Robbie. After all, the child was his nephew. He called long distance directory assistance, wrote the number down, and stared at it a long time. He wanted to dial it so badly that he crumpled it up and threw it away.

After the third time he had enacted this scenario, he realized that he'd memorized the number. Appalled, he strove to forget it. And didn't. Every time he picked up the phone, Nicole's number in Newark ran through his mind like tape in a calculator.

Fortunately, he was busier than ever, the month of June being filled with outdoor shoots. After fifteen years in the business, the past five out on his own, his expertise and reputation had gained him the kind of success he hadn't even dared to dream of when he'd first started out. Everybody wanted Drake Austin, from the leading advertising agencies representing the most successful companies to shoot their print ads to the top magazines to shoot the highest-paid models for their covers. What few spare hours he had, he devoted to assembling a collection of humorous celebrity "outtakes" for a book on photography he'd been contracted to do.

He was turning down assignments other photographers would've killed for because his time was booked solid. And just as often, those he had to turn down told him they preferred to wait for him, rather than hire anyone else.

Not only was he working with the elite, he was partying with the elite. Or he could've been, if he chose. But since that fateful trip to Newark, he returned to his apartment alone after a full day's work and stayed there. Alone. Inevitably, involuntarily, his thoughts would turn to Nicole Fortune. And to her child.

Baby Robbie, Andrew's child. Living in a run-down house in an atrocious neighborhood. Cranky because he didn't like the heat, from which there was no relief in that urban frying pan. There were no trees there, no grass, no swing set in the backyard. There was no yard!

He thought of another child who'd once lived in a crowded, too-hot-in-the-summer-and-too-cold-in-the-winter apartment on the wrong side of the tracks in the small town of Newberry, Pennsylvania. The child that he had been. He hadn't had a yard or a swing set either, but his half brothers had. They'd even had their own swimming pool and cabana!

Sitting alone in his elegant Manhattan living room, Drake remembered the bus ride across town with his mother to the beautiful, spacious home of Preston Austin where the lawn was the biggest and the greenest he'd ever seen. He had never been invited into that house or asked to swim in the pool or play on the lawn, not even after his father had reluctantly introduced him to the rest of the family.

The parallels between his childhood and Robbie's haunted him. Two boys, a generation apart, forced to grow up as poor, illegitimate members of a rich family who could easily support them. But chose not to.

Drake abruptly reached for the telephone. It was too late to help the child he had been, but not too late to give little Robbie the upbringing he deserved. He dialed the number of Preston Austin in Newberry, a small town in Pennsylvania's Lancaster County. The Austin family fortune had been made two generations ago with the large tobacco holdings bought by the first Austins to arrive in the area. Preston Austin's investment savvy had expanded it into the millions.

There had always been an uneasiness between Preston Austin and his eldest son, and this phone call was no exception. Particularly when Drake explained why he was calling.

"Another one?" Preston exploded. "Damn, I can't believe it! That's the third bimbo who's materialized with a kid. It must be some sort of hellish conspiracy. The other two said that the father was named Drake Austin, too, and they wrote your name on the kids' birth certificates. But they had pictures of Andrew and identified him as you, Drake."

Drake paled. He was glad he was sitting down, for otherwise the news would've knocked him off his feet. "Do you mean Andrew fathered two other children, using my name?" His mouth was suddenly, terribly dry. "My God, what are we going to do?"

"Why should we do anything?" Preston laughed harshly. "Andrew is dead. Since his name isn't listed on any of the birth certificates of the little bastards, they're all exempt from his estate. Sure, your name is down, but you're not the father— none of the mothers claim that *you* are. And even if they did, there are certain medical tests which would prove you're not, so you're off the hook, too."

The little bastards. The words rang in Drake's head. "You saw the girls and the children. They had the birth certificates and pictures of themselves with Andrew?" He felt sick.

"Yeah, yeah, so what?" snapped Preston. "Both girls are big-busted airheaded blondes—Andrew's typical choice of broads. How about the one on your end? Same kind of babe, huh?"

Drake thought of Nicole. She was as different from Andrew's typical choice of woman as night was from day. He said nothing, but Preston wasn't really waiting for a reply. "We're not going to do a damn thing, Drake. I scared these two bitches off and I'll send my team of lawyers to run off the one who's hounding you if you can't get rid of her."

"But Andrew really is the father of all three

babies," Drake murmured. He felt as if he were caught in a bad dream. "It was that damn cash incentive you offered, Preston. He was bound and determined to win it. But I never would've thought that even Andrew was capable of using those girls *and my name* to get it."

There was a momentary pause. "You know how jealous Andrew was of you," Preston said soberly. "He was never the same after he . . . found out about you. And maybe I'm partially to blame. I used to use your accomplishments as a way to motivate him . . . Andrew was never the ball of fire you were," he added, as if in justification. "Neither are Dane and Ian, as you well know."

There had been years when he would've sold his soul to hear his father favorably compare him to his half brothers, Drake thought. But it didn't matter now. It was years too late. *The little bastards.* His father's harsh epithet rang in his ears. Was that how his father thought of him, too?

Those so-called little bastards were Preston Austin's own grandchildren; he'd seen the evidence and tacitly admitted it. And if he could turn his back on that particular pair of grandchildren, Nicole, without any kind of proof whatsoever of Robbie's paternity, wouldn't stand a chance to collect.

"What are the children?" Drake heard himself ask in a flat, lifeless voice. "Girls? Boys? One of each?"

"Both girls." Preston laughed. "The deal was a large cash bonus if the child was a boy, remember? So they're automatically disqualified. Andrew must be having a hearty laugh on us from beyond the grave, hmm? Causing all this uproar!"

Drake hung up the phone without another word. His mind was reeling. Andrew had fathered three children—using the name of Drake Austin—and had made no mention of any of the women or provisions for any of the children. Now there were three new members of the Austin clan destined to grow up as outsiders from their wealthy relatives. Who could acknowledge and support them but chose not to.

At the end of June, the temperature in Newark was one hundred four degrees, the highest ever in the past hundred years of the city's recorded weather history. Angry, restless, and hot beyond endurance, teenagers roamed the streets turning on fire hydrants to the delight of the children—and adults—in the neighborhoods.

Hailey took her four-year-old Johnny out to join the water fun while Nicole and Peter stayed inside with the other children and watched from the window. The explosion came without warning. One minute the street was filled with children of all ages frolicking in the water with amused adults looking on, and the next the world seemed to explode around them.

The earth shook and the sounds of shattering glass and frightened screams pierced the air. Nicole dove to the floor, pulling the children down with her. None of them were hurt and all seemed too surprised to cry.

"I wonder what's going on?" Nicole asked in a shaken voice and Peter leaned out the window which was no longer there.

"Fire," he said flatly. "Fire and blood."

Nicole felt chills ripple through her. She dared to rise up and peek out the glassless window frame. The scene in the street made her gasp with horror. It looked like a scene from a war movie massacre. People—bodies?—were lying in the street, in the water which still gushed from the hydrant. Huge billows of dark smoke poured from a point down the block, and the acrid smell was beginning to permeate the air. And then she saw the flames, shooting high into the sky.

"It's the crack house! I—I think it blew up or something." Nicole picked up Robbie and shepherded Peter and the two small children away from the window. "Peter, we've got to find Hailey and Johnny. And we've got to get out of here before the fire spreads!"

Most of the houses on the street, including the crack house, were frame and old, and dry from the extended heat wave. They would go up like boxes of matches lit by a flare, she knew. A cold panic began to seep through her.

It was too much for Peter. He took Demon and resumed his favorite seat beneath the air conditioner in the hall. Which was no longer working. Nicole flicked the hall light switch on and off, confirming her hunch. The electricity was out. The explosion must have ripped through the power lines.

She ran back to the window and looked out. There was pandemonium and panic in the streets. People were running around shrieking and crying, some were bending over the forms lying motionless as the water continued to pour over them. And there was blood. . . . Fire and blood, just as Peter had so cryptically described.

Nicole held Robbie in one arm and with the other drew Hailey's three-year-old Julie and two-year-old Jeffrey close. She couldn't take three little children out into the danger and chaos of the streets to look for Hailey and Johnny. Her eyes flicked up the hall to where Peter sat on the floor, rocking back and forth, the big dog sitting protectively at his side. She couldn't leave the children here, either. Peter simply couldn't cope with looking after them.

The frantic pounding on the front door galvanized her to action. Carrying Robbie and Jeffrey and clutching Julie by the hand, she scrambled down the stairs to open the door. Remondo stood before her, his face a mixture of apprehension and excitement.

"Remondo, have you seen Hailey and Johnny?" she asked before the boy had a chance to speak. "They were out there . . . I have to find them . . ."

"You gotta get outta here!" Remondo exclaimed. "Get Peter and let's go. I found a car." He pointed to the sleek white convertible parked in front of the house. "I already took my mama and my sister away. I'll take you now."

"Not without Hailey and Johnny," Nicole said stubbornly. There was another fierce, booming explosion and the house literally shook. Her face paled. "Remondo, we have to find them. . . ."

"You promise you'll show me how to develop the film?" The dark-haired, blue-eyed beauty playfully tugged at Drake's arm. "This isn't just some dumb come-on to get me into your darkroom? Because if you're going to all this trouble to make a pass—"

"I'd never use a dumb come-on with you, Angelynne," Drake assured her. "And I never make passes in my darkroom. Why take any risks with the film?"

"So you're not just a smooth operator on the make, in the guise of a serious, dedicated photographer?" the girl teased, grinning up at him.

He laughed. "I'm a photographer to the depths of my very soul. Which doesn't mean that I'm not a smooth operator on the make, too."

They burst exuberantly into his office to find Carmen at her desk, staring fixedly at a miniature portable television screen. She glanced up at them and her eyes widened at the sight of the young woman. "Why, you're Angelynne Flynn!"

she exclaimed delightedly. "I know you—you're Kimberly on my favorite soap."

"Which she faithfully watches every day on her lunch hour," affirmed Drake. "Carmen, meet Angelynne Flynn—soap opera ingenue, model, and *Cosmopolitan's* February cover girl. We took the pictures today. Angelynne, this is Carmen Mendez, my invaluable secretary and right arm."

"You haven't been on the show all week," Carmen said to Angelynne. "The last time I saw you, Kimberly and her boyfriend Billy were washed up on an island suffering from amnesia."

"Mmm-hmm." Angelynne laughed. "Doesn't it make you wonder how we both got amnesia? Maybe it's contagious. Actually, Todd Cooper—he plays Billy—and I have two weeks vacation, so Kimberly and Billy are sort of on hold till we get back."

"And she's spending her vacation making lots of extra money modeling," inserted Drake. He smiled at Angelynne. He liked her. They'd met last year when he'd photographed her for a sunglasses print ad—one which had been tastefully but provocatively sexy and had gone on to win an advertising Clio award. "Angelynne sold so many pairs of high-priced sunglasses last year that the company wants us to do a sequel ad this year," he added. "We have it scheduled a few weeks from now out in East Hampton."

He was glad their paths had crossed again. Angelynne was bright, funny, and sexy—and beautiful too, of course—though he placed that attribute below the other three. Most importantly, her personality and presence were strong enough to keep his thoughts from straying to a certain Nicole Fortune. He was determined to stop thinking of her and if that meant spending every spare minute with Angelynne as a diversion, then so be it.

America's most popular, most compelling romance novels...

Here, at last...love stories that really involve you! Fresh, finely crafted novels with story lines so believable you'll feel you're actually living them! Characters you can relate to...exciting places to visit...unexpected plot twists...all in all, exciting romances that satisfy your mind and delight your heart.

EXAMINE 6 LOVESWEPT NOVELS FOR

15 Days FREE!

To introduce you to this fabulous service, you'll get six brand-new Loveswept releases not yet in the bookstores. These six exciting new titles are yours to examine for 15 days without obligation to buy. Keep them if you wish for just $12.50 plus postage and handling and any applicable sales tax. Offer available in U.S.A. only.

"Well, it's lucky you don't have any scenes today, because the local station cut into the middle of the soap with this live news program," Carmen said to Angelynne. "Newark is burning. I've been watching—they're televising it live."

"No kidding?" Angelynne moved around to see the screen. "Wow, look at those flames."

"Somebody firebombed a crack house," said Carmen. "The entire block went up in flames. The firemen had trouble hooking up the hoses because some kids had turned on the fire hydrants earlier so there was a delay in—"

"What part of Newark?" Drake moved closer to the screen. He felt an odd, sickening sense of foreboding which he immediately tried to quash. There must be hundreds of crack houses in Newark, he reasoned. Hundreds! It was absurd for him to suppose that the block on fire could actually be Nicole's and Robbie's.

"Everybody who lives on the block has been evacuated to shelters," Carmen continued. "But there have been quite a few killed already. Thirteen at last count—several of them children." She sighed. "Poor little things."

The newscaster's voice announced in sepulchral tones that another death had been added to the toll: that of a young mother who had been burned while attempting to rescue her child. The little boy was unharmed and had been taken to a shelter by other relatives.

Drake felt his heart jump crazily in his chest. "Where is the fire?" he demanded, and as if in response, the newscaster began to recap the events, beginning with the firebombing of the crack house on Seymour Street.

"Seymour Street?" Drake repeated in horror. No, it couldn't be true. He felt as if he had been suddenly plunged into a living, waking nightmare. *Seymour Street was Nicole's street.* She'd even pointed out the ill-fated crack house to him.

He felt his throat close; his whole body was bathed in a peculiar icy sweat. *A young mother had been killed trying to rescue her child . . .* he knew Nicole well enough to know that she would brave flames for Robbie without a thought for her own safety. His heart seemed to stop and then start again, at a wild, furious pace. The little boy—*Robbie?*—had been taken to a shelter by relatives. *Hailey and Peter?*

"Oh God!" he muttered in a strangled tone and it was more a prayer than an exclamation. Without another word, without another thought for Angelynne or Carmen or anything else, he ran from his office.

Six

Drake considered the drive to Newark—weaving through lanes of traffic at an unconscionable rate of speed, listening to terse news bulletins of the ever-worsening situation in the city—to be the worst trip of his life. But even that paled in comparison to the scene that awaited him upon his arrival at Seymour Street.

The police and firemen were fighting a losing battle at keeping concerned relatives, ghoulish rubberneckers, and ambitious local politicians away from the scene. The news media were camped at one end of the street, incredibly near the flames which had already consumed the entire block and were threatening to spread to the houses beyond.

Drake pushed and shoved his way into the crowd. It was a bizarre, mixed group, some crying, some laughing, some pontificating on the evils of drugs, fires, and crowd control techniques. Eventually, half maddened with impatience and worry, he secured the information he needed: the addresses of the shelters where the neighborhood residents had been taken.

He saw no familiar faces at the first place he tried. But at the next place, the gym of an old elementary school which was filled with lines of cots and chairs, he spied Robbie the moment he entered.

And the split-second relief he felt upon seeing the baby instantly turned into a blood-freezing fear. For Robbie was in Hailey's arms. He was crying, and so was she. So was the other little boy she held in her arms. Her two older children were hanging onto her skirts and crying too. Peter was pacing in a circle around them, mumbling to himself, his pale eyes wide and frightened.

Drake fairly flew across the gym. "Where's Nicole?" he demanded, grabbing Hailey's arm and swinging her around to face him. She was sobbing as if her heart had been broken. The children's cries grew louder and more frantic and Peter covered his ears with his hands and paced faster.

Drake felt sick. Nicole wouldn't have left them here to fend for themselves. They needed her too much. She would be here with them unless . . .

"S-Somebody said that home is whenever you have to go there, they have to take you in," Hailey said between deep sobs. "And no matter what, I always knew the house was there for me and that Nicole would—" Her voice broke and trailed off.

Drake closed his eyes. Her fear and hurt were unbearable to observe. And then there were the children and Peter, whose distress was equally painful to see. An image of Nicole, smiling, her blue eyes flashing with life and intelligence, appeared before his mind's eye, and pain seared him.

Taking a deep breath, he opened his eyes. And saw . . . *Nicole?*

He blinked swiftly, again and again, wondering if he'd lost his mind. But no, crossing the gym, dressed in a rather wilted-looking pair of khaki-colored culottes and matching sleeveless shirt, was Nicole herself, her hair pulled up in a high pony-tail which skimmed her shoulders as she walked.

Her shoulders drooped and her blue eyes glistened with tears. For the first time in her life, she felt truly defeated. She must be losing her grip, Nicole thought, fighting off the urge to throw herself down on one of the cots and cry. Her life had certainly never been problem-free, but she'd always been blessed with the inner resources to deal with problems as challenges rather than crushing obstacles.

But she felt crushed now. Their home was gone and they were here in this horrible, hot gym filled with others whose situations were as miserable and hopeless as their own. And how was she going to tell Peter that she couldn't spring Demon from the animal shelter where he'd been taken because they had no place to put him? They had nowhere to go but here, where animals were strictly prohibited.

Her eyes were fixed on Peter who was still pacing, wild-eyed, possibly hallucinating. One theory on schizophrenia held that it was stress, real or imagined, which triggered a psychotic episode. If that were true, she knew that Peter was going to go over the edge again because losing Demon was the worst possible stress, real or imagined, that could possibly happen to him. The big dog and the unconditional love he offered were often Peter's only refuge from the inner terrors which plagued him.

She choked back the enormous lump which seemed to have taken up permanent residence in her throat. And then her eyes widened, for making his way between the cots, coming directly toward her was . . .

Drake Austin?

She gave her head a slight shake of denial. Good Lord, the stress of the day had unhinged her! Now she was hallucinating, just like Peter. Terrific, she thought wryly. What a perfectly lousy time to find out that I'm schizophrenic too.

"Nicole!"

But it was a very real Drake, not a figmentary one, whose big hands were lifting her up and swinging her around, his face aglow, his light blue eyes shining with relief and unadulterated joy.

"Thank God you're all right!" His voice was husky with emotion. "When I heard about the fire—and then I came here and didn't see you—I thought— Damn, listen to me, I haven't completed a sentence yet!" He laughed at his own incoherence.

Nicole was laughing too. Just the sight of him had sent her spirits soaring into the stratosphere. He set her on her feet, but kept his hands on her waist and continued to gaze at her, as if he couldn't quite trust himself to believe she was really safe. She smiled up at him, her blue eyes bright, her hands resting on his chest.

"You came here looking for us?" she asked softly. A giddy euphoria swept through her, blocking out all the terrible things that had happened today, pushing her earlier desolation and despair back into a far-off corner of her mind. All she could see and think of and feel was Drake.

Who was looking at her in a way that sent a sweet, sensual heat coursing through her. Whose hands tightened around her waist and drew her slowly, inexorably closer to him.

Reflexively, Nicole's hands slid around his neck. A delicious weightlessness made her feel as if she were floating, yet an equally tantalizing pressure in her abdomen made her body swell and ache with longing. Her whole body tingled with life, every nerve sensitive and alive, a wonderful contrast to her earlier deadening depression.

"Did you lose everything in the fire?" Drake asked huskily.

"Not everything. We had some time to grab all the photo albums, some clothes, the children's things, and a few sentimental items that would've been irreplaceable. We dumped them into Remondo's car and he brought us here. It took two trips."

"Remondo managed to get hold of another car?" Drake's lips twisted into a smile. "Whose was it this time?"

Nicole grinned back, her first smile in hours. "I didn't ask."

For several long moments they stared into each other's eyes, each one drinking in the sight of the other. Fear had destroyed the careful walls they'd constructed between them, and their joy at being together again had wiped out every inhibition and reservation. At this moment there was no one else in the world except the two of them. They were as oblivious to their crowded noisy surroundings as they were to the day's grim events.

Drake folded her tightly in his arms and her hands stroked the thick, dark hair at the nape of his neck. Their bodies pressed closer, closer, her soft breasts nestled into the strength of his chest, her belly curving against his middle. They fit together so well, Drake noted dazedly. Their perfect fit in this embrace was erotically evocative of another kind of perfect fit. . . .

Nicole felt his thick masculine tautness move against her and she trembled in response. She clung to him, suddenly feeling too weak to stand. With instinctual, flawless timing, she raised her mouth to him just as he lowered his to her. Her lips were soft and pliant and parted with a soft, shuddering sigh the moment his mouth touched hers.

Their emotions exploded into a wild, hot, and hungry kiss. Nicole felt the moist invasion of his tongue, and passion poured through her in a dizzying wave. She moaned and locked her arms more tightly around him.

They kissed and kissed, deeply, possessively, their tongues mating in an age-old sensual rhythm. Nicole felt a spear of pleasure pierce her so sharply

and so deeply that it reached her womb and re-
leased a sweet flood of desire. She melded her
body to his, her hands caressing him feverishly,
wanting, needing, aching. . . .

"Aunt Nicky, Aunt Nicky!" The high-pitched little voices were too shrill and too near to be ignored. Dazedly, Nicole twisted her mouth away
from Drake's and gazed down at Johnny and Julie,
who were tugging at her and shrieking her name.

"We heard the bell! The ice cream truck is here!"
cried Johnny. "Can we get ice cream, Aunt Nicky?
Mommy says she'll take us out to the truck if you
stay with Uncle Peter."

"I *need* ice cream!" Julie echoed urgently.

Nicole swallowed and tried to stabilize herself. It
wasn't easy. Drake was still clasping her loosely,
but with definite possession. But the magical in-
terlude was over. Everything came back to her in
a rush—the fire, the loss of their home, this de-
humanizing place where they were supposed to
live until God only knew when. The noise and the
heat of the shelter seemed to slam into her with
the force of a runaway train.

She looked down at the hopeful little faces of
Johnny and Julie. She could remember what it
was like being a kid, when the ice cream truck's
stop was the highlight of the day. She was glad
they had something to look forward to. "Sure, I'll
stay with Peter. Go on out to the truck."

The children squealed with delight and headed
toward the door of the gym. Hailey followed them,
pausing for a moment at Nicole's side. She still
held Robbie in her arms, but Jeffrey was on his
feet, pulling at her hand in an impatient attempt
to get to the ice cream truck.

Drake dropped his hands and stepped away from
Nicole. He didn't want to let her go. He wanted to
carry her out of this hellhole and take her some-
place cool and dark and quiet, where they could
be completely alone and undisturbed. His bed-

room would do nicely. Heat suffused him once again. He wanted to take her back into his arms and crush her against him. To open his mouth over hers and thrust his tongue into her mouth, to feel her breasts in his hands, to part her legs and . . .

"I'm sorry, Nicole." Hailey glanced uneasily at Drake and then flushed with embarrassment. "But the kids heard that bell and—"

"You don't have to explain." Nicole laughed shakily. She was careful not to glance in Drake's direction. "Here, I'll take Robbie. You'd better get Jeffrey out there quick before he has a world-class tantrum."

Drake impulsively reached into the pocket of his pale gray slacks. "Use all of this for ice cream," he mumbled, stuffing a bill into Hailey's hand. "The other kids in here might—er—want some."

Hailey stared at the bill, her jaw agape. "A one-hundred-dollar bill!" she squeaked. "I've never ever seen one of these before. Are—Are you sure you don't want change?"

Drake's lips curved into a smile. "I'm sure. Buy as much ice cream for as many kids as you can."

"Thank you!" Hailey beamed, her whole face lighting up. "Thank you so much!"

She was really quite pretty when she smiled, Drake thought, and the sight of her smiling when her young face was streaked with tears moved him. He looked at Nicole who was holding Robbie as she watched Hailey and Jeffrey's happy, speedy exit, and his heart seemed to turn over in his chest.

And alarm bells went off in his head. Is this how it happens? he asked himself nervously. Was this strange melting sensation, this peculiar desire to ease pain and induce smiles . . . was this how Nicole Fortune ended up saddled with a houseful of dependents who needed her? Who were forever making demands on her time and her person?

Why, she couldn't even spend ten minutes kissing him without some of them intruding!

All of his previous trepidations about an involvement with her swamped him in a threatening flood. Along with an unnerving new theory about why she'd become involved with his brother Andrew in the first place. Had Nicole tried to bag Andrew—rich, eligible Andrew—to ensure a life of comfort for her foster kin? From her point of view, having a man's baby must've seemed a sure-fire way to entrap him—and usually was, unless the man was unscrupulous Andrew.

It all seemed to fit. She'd made no pretense of being in love with Andrew, and he knew she was too smart to fall for Andrew's insincere lines. He saw it all now, Drake decided in alarm. Nicole had hoped to land herself a wealthy husband to provide for this motley crew who would undoubtedly depend on her for the rest of their days.

He felt a chill, despite the suffocating heat of the crowded gym. The way she had kissed him, the way she'd aroused him . . . Good Lord, was he the next candidate on her list?

Nicole didn't notice that he was slowly backing away from her, as if she were a lighted stick of TNT. For her eyes were on Peter who was racing up and down the bleachers, talking to himself and gesturing wildly. He was hallucinating, she knew. And others in the gym were beginning to stare at him with expressions varying from curiosity to fear.

"Drake, will you hold the baby for a few minutes? I have to talk to Peter." She thrust Robbie into Drake's arms and rushed off to the top of the bleachers where Peter was standing.

Drake automatically followed her, a wailing Robbie in his arms. The baby had begun to cry again the moment Nicole handed him over. He watched as Nicole tried to talk Peter into taking his medicine, several small pills which she pulled from vials in her purse.

Peter declined the pills. He said it was crack. He asked Nicole why they were all in this crack house, then asked her if she was really Nicole or a crack dealer who was impersonating her.

Nicole turned to Drake with a sigh. "He's delusional—and this time he's fixated on the crack house. When he gets agitated and out of contact like this we have to take him to the hospital and they change his medication. He stays there for a while, until he's no longer psychotic."

She seemed sad but resigned and not at all alarmed. Drake was. He'd never seen anyone delusional and hallucinating. If Peter was unsure of Nicole's identity, if he thought she was a crack dealer, mightn't he try to harm her?

"I'll call the police and ask them to send someone over to take us to the emergency room," said Nicole, starting down the bleachers. She sounded as if this was nothing new, accompanying her psychotic foster brother to the hospital in a police car. And to her, it wasn't.

Drake admired her aplomb. And felt an unexpected wave of sympathy for Peter. He looked years younger than the twenty-six Drake knew him to be, and he seemed so utterly and pathetically confused. Wouldn't the appearance of the police terrify him? In his current state of mind, the poor guy might think he was being mistakenly arrested as a crack dealer himself. Drake imagined Peter resisting the police, being subdued and taken away in handcuffs or something. It seemed so sad. And so preventable.

"Look, do you have to call the police?" Drake heard himself say. "Can't Robbie stay here with Hailey and her kids while I drive you and Peter to the hospital?"

Nicole was too overwhelmed to answer, but the expression on her face said it for her. Her beautiful eyes glowed with appreciation, and she quickly and silently gave him a fierce hug.

Peter was willing to go in the little black Maserati Spyder with Nicole and Drake, whom he recalled as "Remondo's friend." He remembered his previous ride in "Remondo's sports car" too. He was voluntarily admitted to the hospital and gravely assured Nicole that he was on his way to find Demon and that the two of them would then rescue the family from the crack house.

"That poor kid," Drake murmured as he watched Peter accompany the nurse from the emergency room to the psychiatric unit. He looked down at Nicole to see tears sliding down her cheeks.

"It's just not fair!" she cried in a choked voice. "Why does Peter have to be sick? Why can't they find a cure for that damned disease?"

"Oh God, Nicole, don't cry." She certainly had good reason to cry, but seeing her tears cut him to the quick. He pulled her roughly into his arms and held her tightly. "I know you've had a helluva day," he murmured softly. "But please, baby, don't cry."

He felt the way he'd felt the time she had told him that she'd like to sell her house and move her family to a better neighborhood but couldn't. Depressed for her. And trapped by her.

His bachelor's sense of freedom reacted to the threat by wanting to take off. But she was so warm and soft in his arms. And he admired her, respected her too. She didn't crumple and give up in the face of adversity. She just faced it and went on. She fascinated him.

He stroked her nape with his fingers, savoring the soft, silky skin. His other hand was making an independent attempt at comforting her, gliding over her ripely curved figure in a possessive foray. . . .

Drake closed his eyes. He was aware that his caresses were becoming longer and slower. More designed to arouse than to comfort. That his body was reacting to her nearness by growing harder and tighter. That he wanted her very much.

Nicole clung to him, her head resting against his chest, her cheek brushing the soft cotton knit of his shirt. Being held in his arms like this, feeling his warm masculine strength—it was like something out of a dream, she thought dazedly. She couldn't remember the last time she had been held and comforted, probably not since she'd been a small child, for she had become strong and resourceful and dependable quite early in life.

And men didn't cuddle strong, resourceful, dependable women, she was quite aware of that. They ran from them—especially if that woman came equipped with a ready-made family unlikely to ever depart from her life.

For a few minutes, Nicole relinquished her sense of duty and her self-control and allowed herself to luxuriate in Drake's attentions. She pushed the heartbreak of the day from her mind and reveled in the pure pleasure of being close to him. She closed her eyes and breathed in the sexy, musky scent of him, listened to the comforting strong thudding of his heart beneath her ear.

Exhaling on a sigh, she raised her face to him. Her eyes were warm and soft and a brilliant shade of blue. She found him watching her with an intensity that made her pulses run riot.

"Thank you for coming with Peter and me," she whispered. On its own volition, her hand had found its way to his face. She stroked his hard tanned cheek with her slender fingers. "And thank you for buying the ice cream for all the kids in the shelter. It was a wonderful thing to do. You're—" she caught her breath, her emotions sparking her every nerve. "You're the most thoughtful, generous man I've ever met, Drake."

"No." He shook his head in abrupt denial. "I'm not, Nicole. Remember the first time we met? You called me a rat and a rake and you were absolutely right. I am a—"

She silenced him by pulling his head down to her and kissing him with a boldness that would've astonished her in a less emotional state.

Her mouth was sensuous, her lips soft and yielding. Her tongue slipped into his mouth and lured his into the hollow of her own mouth. He filled it, penetrating fully, deeply, in excruciating sexual simulation. His body throbbed, his brain was throbbing too. There was no use denying it, Drake acknowledged with a deep, low groan. He was well and truly trapped. She was backing him into a metaphorical cage—and he was going without a fight.

He knew he wasn't going to let her stay even one night in that awful shelter. His lips nibbled the creamy curve of her neck while his big hands pressed her closer. "You're coming back to New York with me tonight," he said huskily. He pictured the two of them in his bed and a great shudder of desire shook him.

Nicole drew back a little to stare up at him with those captivating blue eyes of hers. "Drake . . ." Her voice shook a little. "Do you mean it?"

He slid his hand lower, to the small of her back and applied the pressure necessary to arch her intimately, provocatively against him. "I mean it, Nicole."

"Oh, thank you!" Nicole cried, hugging him with an exuberance that suddenly was not sexual at all. "We can stop at the animal shelter on our way to the gym and pick up Demon. Oh, Drake, I was afraid we'd never get him back! And then we can go get Robbie and Hailey and the children—I guess we'll have to rent a bigger car, won't we? And then—"

She kept talking and Drake stared at her, in growing alarm. That metaphorical cage door had just clanged shut. He'd made his offer in the heat of the moment, his hormones running on overload. He hadn't thought beyond getting Nicole into his bed. He certainly hadn't given a thought to carting Hailey and all the kids—and the dog!—to New York!

But how could he say no? Nicole looked so happy, so relieved. As if a crushing burden had been lifted from her, and in truth, it had. Despite his reluctance to have the foster Fortunes interjected into his life, he couldn't deny the ripple of satisfaction that accompanied the knowledge that he was the one who'd made her face light up with that breathtaking smile. Had he ever made anyone that happy before in his life?

He knew the answer to that. Of course he hadn't. Detached, uninvolved, mellow cool guys do not exactly bring happiness to others. But the Drake Austin whose hand Nicole gripped as they walked from the hospital to the parking lot was neither detached nor uninvolved, not mellow or cool. And there didn't seem to be a thing he could do to restore his carefully cultivated equilibrium, not with the impulsive and emotional Nicole at his side.

Still, he hadn't reached his level of success without learning how to put up a ferocious fight in his own defense. The cage door wasn't locked yet and he was determined to force it open. Sweet freedom beckoned.

"I just want to get a few things straight between us, Nicole. Now, in the very beginning." He cleared his throat. She was gazing up at him in the most appealing way. He tightened his jaw, purposefully averted his eyes and forged ahead. "I'm not Santa Claus or some kind of wimped-out fairy godfather. I'm not in the habit of giving something for nothing."

Nicole let go of his hand. Drake Austin had the singular ability to make her feel like a yo-yo. Thrown down, jerked back up. It seemed he was about to launch another cycle. "What are you trying to say, Drake?" she asked carefully.

"I expect something in return for providing your unrelated relatives with a roof over their head."

"We'll be glad to pay rent," Nicole shot back.

"I'm not interested in rent money, Nicole. What I want is you in my bed."

A hot blush swept through her as a host of emotions clashed within her. For a few intense moments, she wanted to slap his face for insulting her as much as she wanted to fling herself into his arms and kiss him because he'd just admitted wanting her.

Perhaps he even expected her to do either one, for both were understandable, if not typical feminine reactions to such a remark. Nicole, however, seldom did the expected. Instead, impulsively, she burst into laughter.

Drake stared at her. "What's so funny?" he growled.

"The deal you just offered me." Her blue eyes gleamed. "You'll provide room and board for my entire family if I'll sleep with you? In all fairness, I feel obliged to point out that you're getting the raw end of the deal, Drake. Do you have any idea how much it costs to feed our dog? He literally eats like a horse. And since both Robbie and Jeffrey are still in diapers we spend a small fortune on Pampers. Not to mention the—"

"I didn't ask for an itemized account of your daily living expenses," snapped Drake. "I said I was taking you to bed tonight."

"No." She shook her head. "You're not. If and when we go to bed, it'll be for one reason only— because we're madly in love with each other."

Her voice was wistful, but he didn't notice. He was too incensed by her faux-virginal rules.

"Since when is love a qualification for making love? It certainly wasn't a factor when you hopped into the sack with the late, great Andrew Austin."

He was appalled at the jealousy in his tone. If she were to pick up on it . . .

She didn't. She was too shaken by his reference to Andrew. She'd managed to completely forget that she was supposed to have been Andrew's lover. But Drake never seemed to forget it. And he was bound to catch her in her reluctant deception because she was bound to slip—if they were to spend any amount of time together. Which they wouldn't, not now. Not ever.

"This is never going to work," she said swiftly. "Take me back to the shelter. Hailey's been alone with all the kids long enough. I—appreciate your offer, but I'd better pass on it."

"Pass on it?" he echoed, staring at her, an overpowering ambivalence crashing through him. "Do you mean you're not coming to New York?"

"No, we're not coming. Aren't you relieved?"

"No!"

They stared at each other. "You aren't?" she asked doubtfully.

"What kind of a sociopathic monster do you think I am, Nicole? Do you really think I'd be able to drive blithely off to New York, knowing that you—uh—that my brother's child," he quickly amended, "is stuck in some smelly old gym in the middle of Newark?"

"I won't let you take Robbie," she said quickly, fiercely.

"I know. You've made that very clear. But I can't leave my nephew here. So if I'm to fulfill my avuncular duty to Robbie, I'll have to take his mother, won't I? And since where you go, Hailey and her kids and Peter and the damn dog go—I guess I'm stuck with the lot of you."

He felt much, much better. He wasn't trapped after all. He'd pried open the cage door and he was free! His feelings for Nicole hadn't prompted his invitation, he assured himself. It was his strong sense of responsibility for his baby nephew that caused him to be saddled with the Fortune clan. Nicole just happened to be part of that package, that's all. Pleased, he drew a sigh of relief.

Nicole suppressed a sigh of exasperation. It seemed they were back to being adversaries again. On their way to the animal shelter to reclaim Demon, she decided it was for the best. There was really nowhere for the physical attraction between them to go. If they ever were to fall madly in love—her qualification for sleeping together—he would learn that she'd never given birth to his half brother's son or any other child. He would know that she'd never even gone to bed with a man!

She shivered a little, even though the night air was oppressively warm. Drake would be furious if he found out she'd deceived him about Robbie. He might be angry enough—and vindictive enough— to take him away from her. *No.* Nicole almost shouted it aloud. She squared her shoulders and set her jaw with the determination that had yet to fail her. She would keep her child. She would never let her family be torn apart.

Seven

After one night in his New York apartment with Nicole and kin, Drake took them all to his house in East Hampton. A pony-size dog and four small children definitely belonged in the country, he decided.

He had another, less altruistic reason for moving the group. Spending one night in his apartment with Nicole was an exercise in frustration that he didn't care to repeat. He'd fully intended to take her to bed. He knew she wanted him as much as he wanted her and he didn't anticipate any problems in changing her mind about sleeping with him.

And after the children were settled and the gargantuan dog had been fed and walked and had flopped down near the wall of windows overlooking Central Park, Drake made his move. His mind cloudy with desire, his body throbbing with passion, he set out to entice Nicole into his bedroom.

She was with Hailey, who was crying again. The loss of the house had hit her hard. "What are we going to do, Nicole? Where will we live? We've just joined the ranks of the homeless. What's going to happen to us now?" Hailey cried and cried and asked the same question over and over again.

Drake stood outside the door while Nicole attempted to comfort her. He felt very sorry for Hailey, but he couldn't wait until she fell asleep so he could be alone with Nicole.

Alas, it never happened. Hailey, insecure, tearful and frightened, stuck to Nicole as if she'd been glued to her. Eventually, suffering from an acute case of exasperation and frustration, Drake was forced to abandon his plans for seduction and go to bed. Alone. Where he tossed and turned in a state of restless, unfulfilled desire for most of the night.

Early the next morning, long before most Manhattanites had begun their daily commute, he loaded the entire crew into the rented station wagon, the small U-Haul trailer firmly attached, and drove them to East Hampton, the charming little town on Long Island's South Shore.

His spacious, airy frame house had a wide, long lawn landscaped with flowers, trees, and a carpet of green grass. The property bordered on a stretch of private ocean beach. The urban refugees gazed at their country/surfside surroundings with unconcealed awe.

"I'll be staying at my apartment in the city," Drake told Nicole, after introducing her to Rich and Linda Ruggerio, the thirty-something live-in couple who took care of the place for him. Both Ruggerios were aspiring artists who spent ninety percent of their time painting and the rest on their housekeeping and property-tending chores. Obviously that would change with the arrival of Fortune and Company, and Drake saw the couple stare at the group with horrified consternation.

He couldn't get out of there fast enough. Once he was away from Nicole, the sensual spell she so effortlessly cast over him would weaken and then end, he was certain of that. It had to! In addition, the Ruggerios looked ready to throw a tantrum of major proportions at the unexpected and unwelcome intrusion into their lifestyle.

Back at his office in the city, Drake warned Carmen to expect a call from the Ruggerios at any moment. He wondered who he was going to hire to replace them when they quit in an infuriated huff. Still, he had assuaged his conscience by providing a temporary home for his infant nephew, which was worth the inconvenience of replacing the Ruggerios, he told himself loftily.

But days passed, and the call never came. Had the Ruggerios simply walked off the job without giving any notice at all? What was going on out in East Hampton anyway? His curiosity got the best of him. Enduring the Fourth of July weekend traffic, Drake drove out to see what sort of debacle had ensued.

But he wasn't greeted by a fallout of domestic chaos. To the contrary, the scene was one of domestic bliss. Hailey and her three children were splashing happily in the shallow end of the pool while the dog lazed on a cushioned chaise longue. Rich and Linda sat on the wide, lush lawn, their easels facing the beach as they both worked on impressionistic seascapes.

The wonderful, unexpected aroma of something freshly baked wafted from the kitchen, luring Drake inside. He found Nicole removing two pies from the double oven.

Her face lit up at the sight of him. "Drake!" She rushed over to him, and then remembering the inexplicable and confusing current state of their relationship, stopped in her tracks.

He looked wonderful, she thought, her eyes sweeping over him. His broad shoulders stretched the cotton of his blue shirt over his muscular chest, and his well-worn jeans lovingly molded his masculine contours. Quickly, she averted her gaze and took a deep, bolstering breath.

Drake was staring at her just as intently, taking

in every detail, the way her blue eyes were shining, the luxuriant thickness of her dark hair, the
alluring curve of her lips. She was wearing a bright
yellow blouse knotted at her middle and white
shorts which weren't at all tight or even particularly short, but somehow looked ravishingly sexy
on her.

If the sexual tension in the kitchen had been
measured on a Richter scale, it would've topped
ten.

"We weren't expecting you." Nicole was the first
to break the silence. She silently groaned at her
remark. She sounded as if she were the hostess
in residence and he was an errant drop-in guest.
It would serve her right if he verbally annihilated
her.

But he didn't. "I know Linda didn't bake those,"
he said dryly, pointing at the pies. "Her idea of
dessert is breaking open a bag of Oreos."

Nicole grinned. "We found a whole patch of black
raspberry bushes. I put up some preserves and
made these pies and—" she broke off with a breathless laugh. "I hope you like black raspberries. Rich
says he's going to turn into one, he's eaten so
many these past few days. We're going blueberry
picking next. He likes those better." She couldn't
seem to stop talking. She felt ridiculously shy and
uncharacteristically self-conscious in his presence.

Rich. Drake picked up on that at once. "Sounds
like one big, happy family out here. To think I
actually thought there might be some adjustment
problems."

"Oh no. We're very adaptable," she assured him.
"We could live anywhere with anyone."

His eyes raked over her. "I don't doubt that for a
minute." Hadn't she once intended to take on
Andrew and his sizable income? She would've undoubtedly made a go of living with him, if need
be.

Drake's sardonic tone and the sudden coldness

in his eyes made her uneasy. "I—I hope you're staying for the weekend," Nicole said, the words tumbling from her lips in a rush. "There's going to be fireworks tomorrow. Rich and Linda said they'd take the kids to see them." A timer buzzed, interrupting her. She quickly moved to the stove and removed a pot of parboiled potatoes from the burner. "I'm making potato salad for dinner tonight. We're having fried chicken and fresh tomatoes too. You are staying for dinner, aren't you?" She knew she was talking too much again. Finally, mercifully, she had to pause to breathe.

"You're doing the cooking?" He knew the answer before he asked the question. The meals Linda served came wrapped in plastic, the faster to be defrosted in the microwave.

"I love to cook. And Linda is so busy with her painting, she—" A familiar infantile wail interrupted her. "Oh, that's Robbie waking up from his nap."

Drake followed her out to the long, screened-in porch which spanned the back of the house. Wearing diapers and a cotton T-shirt, Robbie was sitting up in a playpen, rubbing his eyes and complaining vigorously. He broke into a huge grin the moment he saw Nicole.

Drake watched her pick him up and cuddle him. The scene worked its usual magic on him. She was beautiful and the baby was beautiful and watching the two of them filled him with a longing he couldn't deny.

But he made a good try. The cage was looming again. "Where did this thing come from?" he asked gruffly, indicating the playpen. "It sure as hell doesn't belong to me."

"Rich borrowed it from a friend of his. He got us cribs for Jeffrey and Robbie, too. He and Linda have been terrific, Drake. We feel like we're old friends already."

Drake arched his brows. "I see."

"We've been having a wonderful time here," she said softly, her eyes earnest and sincere. "It's been the vacation of a lifetime for us. I'll never be able to thank you enough."

The vacation of a lifetime. Her words touched him. He'd always considered this place merely a pleasant alternative to the city. "A few days in East Hampton is hardly the vacation of a lifetime," he refuted dryly. "A trip around the world with first class accommodations all the way is the vacation of a lifetime. And there *is* a way you can thank me if you're so inclined," he added.

He'd intended to sound teasing; the serious intensity of his tone astonished him.

Nicole's heart jumped. "Go to bed with you, you mean?" She swallowed. "Would you really want me under those circumstances, Drake?"

"Are there fireworks on the Fourth of July? Is the Pope Catholic? Yes, Nicole, I'd take you under those circumstances."

She decided he was kidding. He had to be. "I don't believe you," she teased back. "You're the guy with the World-Trade-Center-size ego, remember? You couldn't stand knowing that the only reason a woman slept with you was out of gratitude. You wouldn't settle for anything less than complete adoration on her part."

"Oh, how wrong you are." Drake's laugh was positively unholy. And sexy. He took Robbie from her and set the baby in the playpen. Robbie's gaze happened to land on a brilliant pink toy pig and he reached for it, momentarily forgetting that he was back in the pen.

With a slow sure ease, Drake caught Nicole's hand and pulled her toward him. "Care to test your theory, baby? I'll have you in bed by the count of five. One."

His arms encircled her in the same moment that his mouth covered hers. Nicole felt her eyes closing and didn't try to fight the blaze of sensual heat that seared through her. She'd spent every night here in his house thinking of him, dreaming of him, wanting him. She'd gone into his bedroom and imagined the two of them entwined and passionate on the outrageously large bed with its chocolate-brown spread and big brass headboard.

And now he was here, warm and hard and strong, holding her, kissing her, wanting her. Her breasts swelled, her belly tightened, her loins ached. She wrapped her arms around his neck and melted against him.

His tongue was in her mouth and she felt its arousing effects down to her toes, which curled in her sandals. She touched her tongue to his, stroked it, and heard a low groan emanate from deep in his throat. He thrust a denim-clad thigh between her legs and curved his big hands around the rounded firmness of her bottom, molding her intimately to him. Nicole felt a bolt of sensual electricity that sent streaks of pleasure along the insides of her thighs.

His mouth left hers to trail a string of fiery kisses along the sensitive, silken curve of her throat. "You smell good," he said unsteadily. His head was reeling. She felt so good in his arms. He took a gentle love bite of the creamy softness of her neck, then sensuously soothed the area with his tongue. "You taste good too." His voice was a husky, sexy growl. "Sweet. You're so sweet, Nicole. And so responsive."

He moved his hands to her midriff, bared by the knotted blouse. He kneaded the slender curve of her waist, relishing the texture of her smooth skin.

"Oh, Drake." Nicole buried her face in the curve of his shoulder, inhaling the arousing, masculine scent of him. She could feel the taut shape of him straining against the fabric of his jeans.

"Let me have you, sweetheart," Drake murmured

deeply. "It'll be good, baby, the best you've ever had."

At that very moment, Robbie, with impeccable timing, tossed his toy pig out of the playpen. "Uh-oh!" He proudly enunciated his only word of English. When neither adult responded, he reverted to his own language to vociferously demand the return of his pig.

Nicole pulled herself out of Drake's arms. She was breathing heavily and her lips were moist and swollen from his kiss. In one swift movement, she picked up the baby and the toy, turning her back to Drake.

"How far did you count?" she asked in a quavering voice she scarcely recognized as her own. Her own vulnerability and the force of her desire for Drake stunned her. Frightened her too. For those few minutes in his arms she'd forgotten that he was on an ego trip, trying to get her into bed because she'd refused him. Nor had she remembered the critical fact that she dare not ever sleep with him.

There had been nothing but the two of them sharing a very special, private moment with nothing between them but their love for each other.

Nicole gave her head a shake. *Their love? Oh come on now, Nicole,* she silently berated herself. Drake Austin didn't love her. Good Lord, she was beginning to think scarily like Cheryl, eagerly convincing herself that the man she wanted loved her. Because she was in love with him?

No, she couldn't be. She denied it with silent, prompt vigor. She'd never done anything irrevocably stupid in her entire life, and falling in love with the unattainable Drake Austin definitely qualified as irrevocably stupid. She was dazzled by him, by his good looks and his aura of wealth and power and success. And she was profoundly grateful to him—after all, he had rescued her family from that godawful shelter and provided them with the most luxurious, carefree week of their lives.

But she was not about to fall victim to some stupid Cinderella syndrome and fall in love with the handsome prince. She'd always preferred the make-it-happen fairy godmother in that tale. That was her own role in real life. The Haileys and Cheryls of the world inevitably played Cinderella, waiting to be rescued by the man of their dreams. But not Nicole Fortune.

What was she thinking? Drake wondered, staring at the tempting, vulnerable curve of her nape. He closed the small distance between them and wrapped his arms around her middle, his fingers caressing the soft white skin of her bare midriff.

"I wasn't counting, Nicole," he murmured, brushing her nape with his lips. He closed his eyes as a wave of longing crashed through him. "I wasn't thinking of anything but how much I want you."

Nicole tried to wiggle out of his grasp. "You just want me because I said no. You think I'm deliberately challenging you—but I'm not."

He didn't let her go. "You're not?" He nibbled on her neck, enjoying the fresh scent of her hair, the unique taste of her skin. "I know you want me, but you insist on playing hard to get. I'd call that a challenge."

She tried to concentrate on Robbie, contentedly gnawing the ear of his pig as she held him in her arms. But all she could feel was Drake's solid frame close behind her, the strength in his arms, and the sensual expertise of his fingers on her bare skin. The moist warmth of his mouth on her neck sent a syrupy heat flowing through her.

"I'd call it self-preservation," she said shakily. "I can't have an affair with you, Drake. It would never work out. We're too different. It . . . it would be disastrous." It would mean everything to her, while he would consider it a passing diversion, at best. And at worst, an enraging deception.

"You're too serious, Nicole. Sweetheart, you have to learn to lighten up. Enjoy the moment without cluttering it up with a lot of emotional baggage. I can make you feel better than you've ever felt in your life. And—"

"Thank you, Drake." Catching him completely off guard, she jerked out of his arms. "I admit that my willpower was starting to fade, but you revived it with that nauseating live-for-the-moment garbage. For future reference, in your future flings stick with actions and skip the words."

He flushed. "I thought it was worth a try," he grumbled. "It might've worked, you know."

"Not a chance—not with me!" She turned to face him, a derisive smile on her lips. "Yuck! It was like listening in on some bozo making a move on Cheryl." Unfortunately, Cheryl invariably found such lines highly exciting and romantic and succumbed to them. Nicole frowned.

"Bozo?" Drake repeated, his color deepening. "First you call me a jerk, and now a bozo?" He glared at her. "Your tongue is as sharp as a razor blade, Miss Fortune. Furthermore, you're the *only* person who's ever called me either a jerk or a bozo—which says something about *you*, not me."

"Uh-huh. It says I'm honest and you're surrounded by self-serving sycophants. You know, fellow jerks and bozos."

"That's not true!" His voice rose. In a volatile compounding of emotions, anger joined the passion coursing through him. He reached for her and she barely managed to slip away. He made another grab for her. "You're a sanctimonious, self-righteous, manipulative little—"

"Whoa! Wait a minute, my man!" Rich Ruggerio admonished, inserting himself strategically between Drake and Nicole. They had both been so absorbed in their quarrel that neither had noticed him join them on the porch.

"What's going on here, Drake?" demanded Rich.

"I've never seen you so uncool in all the time that I've known you. You looked like a maniac, man. Screaming and lunging at poor little Nicole. And her with a baby in her arms! You're going to scare her to death!"

"I'm not afraid of Drake," Nicole said quickly. "And—And he had every reason to be furious with me, Rich. I was deliberately provoking him."

"Yeah?" Rich stared curiously from one to the other. "Why?"

Nicole clamped her teeth over her lower lip. "It's personal, Rich. Between Drake and me."

"Well, if you say so." Rich shrugged. "Uh, is the laundry done? I want to change into my running gear."

"It's folded on your bed." Nicole smiled at him, and Rich beamed back.

"Hey, thanks, Nicole." He turned to Drake and laid a fraternal hand on his arm. "Go easy on her, huh, buddy? This is one terrific gal. She and Hailey are the best guests you've ever brought out here. It's a real pleasure having them."

"You didn't think so when you first met them," Drake reminded him sourly.

Rich flashed a sheepish grin. "My mistake. They're superfection, they're unparalleled. They take total responsibility for their kids and dog. They do the cooking and cleaning and the laundry—and cheerfully too! Hailey's even getting interested in tending the flowers. Great group, Drake. I hope they stay the whole summer." With that, he dashed into the house.

"Quite a testimonial," Drake said drolly. "I'm wondering why I should keep the Ruggerios here. They seem superfluous at this point."

"They're serious artists. They need time for their art," Nicole explained. "And Hailey and I don't mind doing the housework. It's really no more than we did at home—and under far more pleasant conditions." She exhaled on a sigh. "Drake, I really don't think you're a jerk or a bozo. I just said it because . . ."

"I was behaving like a jerk and a bozo?" Drake suggested.

She laughed. "Well, maybe just a little."

"Who's Cheryl?" he asked suddenly.

Nicole's eyes widened. "One of my foster sisters." She glanced down at Robbie and her arms tightened instinctively. "One who's had more than her share of jerks and bozos in her life. Not to mention the downright creeps and users. I—I'm afraid she's involved with one of those now."

"Does that mean she'll be turning up at the door with a passel of kids?" Drake asked in mock alarm.

"I'm afraid she's going to turn up in a triple X-rated movie in VCR's across the country." Nicole's brows narrowed. "She says she's in an art film that Thad Griffin's producing, but not directing. In fact, his name isn't to be connected with the movie at all, but he expects to make a lot of money from it. If you knew Cheryl and her history with men, those circumstances would make your blood run cold."

"I know Griffin. To my knowledge he's never done porn . . . on-screen, anyway. Off-screen, he's been known to be—er—somewhat debauched at times."

"You know him?" Nicole repeated, her blue eyes brightening. "Oh, Drake, maybe you could call him and find out about this movie! I've tried calling Cheryl, but I keep getting this answering machine that fires off a string of rude one-liners. I don't know where she's living or what's she's doing. I've left this phone number on the smart-alecky answering machine, but I don't know if she's gotten the message."

"Nicole, I don't know Griffin well enough to call and ask him if he's clandestinely producing pornography. I did a few stills of him about ten years ago, when he was starring in a movie. Before he started directing. One of them went on to become a million-selling poster."

"So he knows who you are. If you called him, he'd at least return your call," insisted Nicole. "You wouldn't have to mention the movie at first, just ask him about Cheryl and—"

"Oh, yeah, I can hear that conversation now." Drake rolled his eyes and laughed sardonically. "It would go something like this: 'Say, Thad, old pal, you haven't heard from me in the past decade, but I thought I'd give you a call to ask if you're using my girlfriend's sister in a porn flick you're secretly making. I guess you're producing it for some necessary, quick bucks since the IRS and the INS are both on your tail, huh?' "

My girlfriend. The phrase echoed in Nicole's head, and she didn't hear another word he said. His girlfriend. He'd been referring to her.

Drake saw the expression on her face and instantly recalled his slip of the tongue. "I could've said the mother of my nephew, but it was too cumbersome," he said defensively. "In case you didn't get my drift, I was being sarcastic."

"I know," she said quickly. "We both know I'm not your girlfriend."

"At thirty-five, I don't have girlfriends, anyway. I have affairs with women."

"Yes, lots of affairs. With plenty of sex but no real involvement or commitment. Because you want relationships limited to the physical, without any emotional ties. Because emotions pose a threat to the pseudocool facade you've built to hide behind."

"You're hardly one to deliver sermons, Nicole. You're a regular Machiavellian princess with all your plots and plans and schemes."

"I don't know what you're talking about," she retorted hotly.

"Don't insult me by playing dumb, Nicole. You're anything but that. I know all about you and Andrew, remember? And I know you used him as much as he used you. Both of you were in it for the money—he to collect Preston Austin's grandchild cash bonus award and you to provide a cushy lifestyle for your innumerable relatives. Now you've got your eye on me . . . you've already admitted how much you like it here and—"

She didn't bother to stick around to hear the rest. Nicole fled from the porch, Robbie in her arms. Drake watched her make her way to the swimming pool where Hailey and her children were playing and wondered why he was feeling so guilty.

She avoided him for the rest of the day. She didn't speak to him at all during dinner, though he repeatedly tried to engage her in conversation. He even complimented her on the dinner—the fried chicken and potato salad qualified as the best he'd ever had and the pies were nothing short of fantastic. He told her so, but she wouldn't even glance in his direction.

Hailey, Rich, and Linda didn't seem to notice that he was being snubbed. Or if they did, they didn't care, for they conversed happily among themselves and the children. And with Nicole. She was affable and pleasant to *them*.

After dinner, Rich and Linda took off on their bikes to visit some friends while Hailey and Nicole cleaned up the kitchen. The children played on the porch within view of their mothers and the ever protective Demon.

Drake prowled through the house, feeling out of sorts. And mightily abused. Why should *he* feel like an outsider in his own house? he mused irritably. He'd merely told Nicole a few home truths—something she had no compunction about doing to him.

He stayed out of the way until the children were bathed and put to bed, then joined Hailey and Nicole on the big, old-fashioned front porch where they sat in cushioned wicker chairs, sipping cool drinks.

"That looks good," he said congenially, nodding at the pitcher of iced lemonade. "I think I'll have a glass."

Nicole stood up and went into the house, as silent and stone-faced as a statue. Hailey jumped to her feet and poured a glass of lemonade. "Here you are, Drake," she said nervously, handing it to him. "We made it fresh. Rich and Linda like it better than iced tea or iced coffee."

"Rich and Linda have been leading a life of ease this past week," Drake remarked, sitting down on the wicker love seat. "Have they done a damn thing around here since you arrived?"

Hailey slowly sank back into her seat. She looked as if she would've preferred to run. "We're glad they like us. It can't have been easy for them, having all of us dumped on them without any notice."

"You're quoting your sister, of course. Nicole," he added, fairly spitting out the name.

"Nicole always knows the right things to do and say to make things work out for us," Hailey said eagerly. "She always has."

Drake scowled. "I didn't phrase it quite that way, but I said much the same thing to her this afternoon and she hasn't spoken to me since."

"I wonder why?" Hailey looked bewildered. "It's true, I've often told her so. Her mother Anne is a sweet lady who took all of us kids in and loved us to pieces, but it was Nicole who knew how to make it work out as a family. We were a sad, disturbed bunch and Anne's sweetness wasn't enough. Nicole is as loving as her mother, but she's practical and tough too. She kept the wild kids in line and protected the weak kids."

Hailey heaved a sigh. "Now, there's only Cheryl, Peter and me left—one wild and two weaks. Poor

Nicole. She must wonder if she'll ever be rid of us."

Drake saw Nicole's shadow in the hall. Was she going to come back out? To lure her, he attempted to draw Hailey into conversation. "Where's your husband, Hailey?" he asked conversationally, casting an expectant eye toward the door. "Do you hear from him often?"

"He's somewhere out west." Hailey studied the wooden slats of the porch, her voice soft and sad. "He notified me that he'd gotten a quickie divorce in Nevada last month and that he was moving on. We don't have his address."

"Is he faithful about sending child support?"

Hailey shook her head. "Somehow he doesn't have to pay any. Nicole said it's because he lied and said he didn't have any children. I don't know if he did. All I know is that I have a copy of the divorce decree and it doesn't mention child support."

"That's outrageous!" Drake exclaimed. "I can just imagine how Nicole reacted to that. Why don't you track him down? It's a father's duty to support his children, Hailey."

"It would cost too much to hire a private detective." Her eyes filled with tears. "I just can't understand how he could leave the kids like that. I love them so much—all I've wanted since I was a little girl was to be a mother. I was one of the few orphans in foster care," she added rather proudly. "I came to the Fortunes because my parents were killed in a car accident, not because I was taken from a horrendous home by Child Welfare. I always knew I'd be a good mother and I am. I just wish I wasn't so scared all the time." Her voice broke on a sob. "I wish I could go out and make it on my own with my kids but it seems impossible. I'm afraid my kids and I will always be a burden on Nicole, just like Peter. And Cheryl too."

Drake was nonplussed. "I'm sure Nicole doesn't consider any of you a burden," he said soothingly.

"No, I know she doesn't. But we are. Me with my three kids. Peter with his illness. And who knows when Cheryl will show up on the doorstep with another baby? It'll probably be Thad Griffin's child this time—she's so pitifully naive."

The front door banged open and shut again, and Nicole stood on the porch. "Hailey, I think I heard Jeffrey calling you."

Hailey hopped to her feet, and with a slightly apologetic smile at Drake, hurried inside.

Drake stood up too. "Nicole," he began.

She gave him a look that could freeze fire, turned on her heel and left him standing alone.

Eight

She couldn't have chosen a more effective way to torture him, Drake lamented, casting a covert glance at Nicole over the breakfast table the next morning. Her silence had lasted through yesterday evening, despite his four—*four!*—futile attempts to break it. His fifth attempt, when he'd gone to her bedroom at midnight, had been unsuccessful as well. He'd turned the knob, only to find the door locked. And though he'd called her name in a whisper, there had been no response. Of course, she could've been sleeping . . . but he was positive she hadn't been.

Damn, she was stubborn! He reluctantly marveled at the force of her will. He was congenitally unable to sustain a long period of silence, and he conceded that her refusal to speak to him was driving him out of his mind. Drastic measures were called for.

He approached her again later that morning when she was standing in the shallow end of the swimming pool, dipping Robbie into the water. The baby squealed and splashed with pleasure.

His eyes roved hungrily over her, taking in the curves of her full breasts, small waist, and rounded hips displayed to perfection in the modestly cut black-and-green maillot swimsuit which he recognized as Linda Ruggerio's. But the suit had looked entirely different on Linda's bony, angular figure. Drake swallowed hard. "I want to talk to you," he said with what he considered remarkable restraint.

She ignored him, as if he weren't there.

"Dammit, Nicole, how long is this going to go on?" He protested plaintively. "You can't live under my roof and never speak to me again!"

Nicole spoke then. And her words cut into him with the force of a machete. "Are you telling us to leave? All right, we'll go." Holding Robbie with one arm, she began to climb the ladder out of the pool.

Drake fixed his eyes on her legs. They were long, supple, shapely. "I didn't say anything about anyone leaving," he said tightly.

Nicole didn't appear to hear him. "I'll get our things together immediately. I'm sure Rich or Linda will be kind enough to drive us into town."

Hailey, standing nearby and watching her children play on the grass with a plastic beach ball, stood up, her dark eyes filled with panic. "Nicole, where will we go? What—"

"We'll go back to Newark, of course," Nicole said firmly.

"No!" Drake's hands closed around her shoulders. "You're not going anywhere. Now stop scaring Hailey. This is our own private war and it's not fair to drag anyone else into it."

She gave him a baleful glance and moved away from him. Keeping up her anger was an excellent way of concealing her pain. She didn't want him to know how much he'd hurt her with his accusation yesterday. He already knew way too much about her. He knew how quickly he aroused her, how much she wanted him. If he were to couple that knowledge with the realization that his insulting words had caused her heart-shattering pain, why, he would think . . . he would think . . .

Nicole turned away from him, wrapping Robbie in a towel and patting him dry. She didn't want to think what he would think!

"I called Thad Griffin this morning," Drake said, and Nicole nearly dropped Robbie, so great was her surprise. For a full moment, she could only gape at him.

Drake felt a surge of triumph. Ha! He knew that would get her attention. Little Miss Fortune would talk to him now. "And I asked about Cheryl," he added grandly.

"W-what did he say?"

Drake's smile faded somewhat. "He agreed to pay Cheryl's airfare back to Florida. He promised to get her her job back at the jewelry boutique, too. As of now, she's out of the—er—film."

"Then it really was a slimy porno movie!" cried Nicole. "Oh, Drake, thank you, thank you for getting her out of it. What did you say to Griffin to make him let her go?"

Drake grimaced. "You don't need to know, Nicole."

"You threatened him?" Nicole guessed, wide-eyed.

Drake shrugged. "I'd rather not discuss it." Never would he admit that he'd told Griffin that his "girlfriend" was concerned about her sister Cheryl and wanted to make sure that the movie she was in was a legitimate, respectable film. Griffin, not wanting to offend one of the country's leading photographers, had tactfully agreed to send Cheryl back east that very day. No further mention was made as to the nature of the film. There was little point in stating the obvious.

"I—I'm very grateful for your help," Nicole said quietly, praying that he wouldn't spoil everything by making some biting sexual innuendo about how to repay favors. To her relief, he didn't.

Encouraged, she went on. "Cheryl had a terrible life before she came to live with us. She was sexually abused by a string of her mother's boy-friends before she was put in her first foster home. By then, she was alternately seductive and dis-trustful with men. They placed her with us when she was eleven, after she'd been molested in two previous foster homes. When she was thirteen, she discovered boyfriends and she's never been without one since. They've all used her and taken advantage of her. It's like she feels she doesn't deserve to be treated any better."

"That's an appalling story. I'm glad I intervened with Griffin."

"I am too, Drake," Nicole said quietly.

He cleared his throat. "I don't feel like hanging around the house today, but the town will be mobbed with people in for the holiday. I was think-ing about driving out to Montauk State Park. It's on the farthest point of Long Island and hopefully won't be mobbed with tourists. Do you—uh—care to come along?"

She wanted to go with him so much she could hardly speak. She gazed at him, unable to conceal the longing in her eyes. "Yes," she said softly. "But I'll have to pack a bag for the baby first."

The baby. He wasn't expecting to bring the baby along. Then he looked at Robbie's cheerful gummy grin and big, bright eyes and decided he didn't mind. "Okay. Get out of that wet suit and get his things together and then we'll leave."

She quickly changed into a pair of cutoff jeans and a T-shirt with a decal of the flag ironed on it. She'd bought it in high school and had worn it on every July Fourth since. After changing Robbie into a red-and-white sunsuit, she filled the diaper bag, packed a picnic lunch, and joined Drake on the front porch.

They stuck strictly to neutral, impersonal small talk on the drive to Montauk. Both were aware that a truce was in effect. And both were relieved that the hostility between them was in abeyance.

In fact, they got along amazingly well during their trek through Montauk State Park, the ten-mile strip of woodlands, stark cliffs, dunes, and white beaches which jutted into the ocean. They walked to the point at the tip of the peninsula and gazed out at the whitecapped waters of the Atlantic Ocean. They viewed the Montauk Light-house, built far back in 1795.

They took turns carrying Robbie, and Nicole instructed Drake in how to change the baby's diaper, a lesson which caused them both to dissolve into fits of laughter. Since they'd brought a lunch of cold fried chicken, rolls, fruit and cookies, they had a picnic in the park, under a leafy, thick-trunked tree.

After eating, Nicole gave the baby a bottle of juice and laid him down on the blanket to nap. They sat quietly, listening to the rustle of the leaves and the lapping of the waves against the shoreline as Robbie drifted off to sleep.

"He's sound asleep," Drake observed, gazing at the baby with a smile. "All this fresh air must've tuckered him out."

Nicole heaved a relaxed sigh. "I'm so tired I could fall asleep too. I was awake half the night last night. . . ." Too late she remembered whom she was confiding in. The cause of her sleepless night himself.

Drake wasn't about to let her slip pass without comment. "Why couldn't you sleep last night, Nicole?" His voice fairly dripped with concern. "Was your room too hot?"

"It can never get too hot, not with the ceiling fan and the ocean breezes."

"And if the fan and the breeze don't make it cool enough, you could close the windows and turn on the air conditioner," Drake reminded her. "So . . . if it wasn't the heat, what kept you awake, Nicole?"

"You know very well." She stared at him, her

blue eyes flickering with humor. "You just want to hear me say it."

"Hey, remember the size of my ego? You bet I want to hear you say it."

She inhaled sharply. "I couldn't sleep because I was too upset. I—I hate it when we fight, Drake," she added, her voice lowering to a whisper. She looked away from him, studying the weave on the blanket. "And we seem to do it all the time."

"We only fight to keep from doing what we really want to do, Nicole." He cupped her chin with his hand and tilted her head upward, making her meet his eyes. "And you know what that is, don't you?"

Her mouth trembled as she tried to smile. "Do you mean if we were to make love we'd find ourselves in a state of perfect harmony? No more arguments or quarrels or snapping at each other? I don't think I believe that, Drake."

"Believe it, Nicole. It's the unresolved sexual tension that has us at each other's throats. Basically we like each other very much."

"I know." She sighed again. "I think we could be very good friends if—" A slow blush colored her cheeks.

"If we didn't have the hots for each other," Drake finished. "And while we're on the subject . . ." He slowly, leisurely lowered her down onto the blanket. "All this talk about sexual tension and making love is turning me on. What about you?"

He lay down beside her, resting on one propped elbow, his other hand placed possessively on her stomach. The warm, hard feel of his hand and the sensual gleam in his pale blue eyes sent a ribbon of desire snaking through her.

Her eyes met and held his. "I . . . we . . . the baby . . ." she whispered, her voice breathless.

Her incoherent answer made him smile. "Relax, Nicole. Much as I'd like to, I know we can't strip off our clothes and make love with the baby sleeping two feet away from us. But we can kiss, can't we? For just a little while?"

She sighed and reached up to wrap her arms around his neck. "Yes," she breathed. "Oh, yes. Kiss me, Drake."

"Nicole," he groaned into her mouth and he kissed her, hard and fierce and deep, as if he were starving for the taste of her. She shivered, despite the warm summer heat, and responded without hesitation, her mouth open and hungry under his.

His hand closed over her breast, and she could feel the warmth and the strength of it through the cotton of her shirt and the lacy sheerness of her bra. A soft moan escaped from deep in her throat and she arched into his palm in unconcealed sensual need. His fingers found her nipple, and even through the cloth felt its taut peak.

"I want to see you," he rasped against her lips. Before she could think or speak or even breathe, he pushed up her T-shirt and unclasped the front fastener of her bra, pushing it away to bare her breasts.

"You're beautiful," he murmured as he gazed down at her swollen, milky-white breasts with their tight pink tips. "Do you know how many times I've wanted to see you like this? How often I've fantasized about this . . ."

He circled her nipple with his thumb, and the sensation that spun through her was shattering in its intensity. "Beautiful," he said again, his eyes drinking in the sight of her. His other hand went to the snap of her jeans and he toyed with it. One long finger slipped inside and traced along the elastic waistband of her panties before dipping into the hollow of her navel.

Nicole sucked in her breath. The feelings coursing through her were stronger and more exquisitely pleasurable than anything she'd ever experienced in her life. She felt a wanton urge to put his hands on her breasts and press herself against him. Her knees flexed deeply and she felt a hot, achy pressure between her thighs. Instinctively, she arched her hips upward, trying to meet his finger, which still toyed with her navel. She wanted him to slide it lower, to touch her in the place which was throbbing and moist and so very hot. . . .

And then he withdrew his hands and sat up on the blanket, his back to her. Disoriented from the abrupt cessation of passion, Nicole lay on her back, her breathing heavy, her heart thundering in her ears.

Drake reached down and pulled her to a sitting position beside him. Keeping one arm around her shoulder, he fastened the clip of her bra with his other hand and pulled down her shirt. Nicole leaned her head against his shoulder, her face hot with color.

"I'm sorry," she whispered. "I never meant to let things get that far."

"I should be apologizing to you, Nicole. I'm not a high school hotshot out to score. I only meant to kiss you, but when I had you in my arms all my good intentions just melted away. You go to my head like a jug of one-hundred-proof moonshine."

She slipped her arm around his waist. "That's funny. You affect me exactly the same way."

They sat together, their arms around each other, listening to the peaceful sounds of the countryside. Robbie stirred and turned in his sleep.

"This is the wrong time and the wrong place for us to make love, Nicole," he murmured, touching his lips to her temple. "But we're going to be together very soon. You know that, don't you?"

"We can't let it happen, Drake." She sat up straight, her body rigid with tension, her voice trembling with urgency. "Oh, if only I could explain . . ."

"Explain what, sweetheart?"

She bit her lip, wanting desperately to confide in him. "There's so much at stake," she murmured, half speaking her thoughts aloud. "I can't risk it. I don't dare."

He gazed into her troubled blue eyes. "Nicole, does what you're saying have anything to do with Andrew?"

She nodded, her mouth dry. It had *everything* to do with Andrew—and the fact that she'd never even met him, let alone slept with him. That she was not the mother of his child, Drake's nephew.

"And you're afraid it'll disturb me," Drake surmised.

"More like shock you," she amended. Would it ever!

"I have some shocking news about Andrew myself." Drake rubbed his hands over her slender shoulders and pulled her closer. "This isn't going to be easy for you to hear, Nicole. I don't even know if I ought to tell you."

Her curiosity was piqued. "You can't *not* tell me now, Drake."

"Nicole, Robbie wasn't the only child Andrew fathered in the months before his death. Apparently, he was absolutely determined to win that money our father was offering. There were two other women . . . and each one has a baby girl, around the same age as Robbie."

"You mean Robbie has two half sisters?" Nicole was flabbergasted. "Andrew made *three* women pregnant? Why, the man was a walking sperm bank!"

Drake stared at her. Her reaction to the news of her philandering lover's other offspring puzzled him. But then she'd never claimed to have been in love with Andrew. He frowned. Something here was not quite right. The person he knew Nicole to be didn't take sex casually—Lord knows she took *nothing* casually!

Nicole prodded him for information about the

two other women that the mercenary Andrew had impregnated for financial gain. She wondered how much like Cheryl they were, and from Drake's description of them via his father she concluded that they were virtual Cheryl clones. She felt incensed on their behalf.

"It's so unfair!" she cried. "Why do men like Andrew always hone in on the Cheryls of the world? They seem to have radar! What are those poor girls going to do?"

"The two other mothers remind you of Cheryl?" Drake asked in bewilderment.

Nicole nodded vigorously. "Right down to the blond hair, the buxom chest, and the air heads."

"Andrew's type of woman." Drake arched his brows. "But you aren't, Nicole. In fact, the longer I know you and the more time I spend with you, the harder it is to imagine the two of you together. Andrew demanded subservience and blind worship from a woman and I can't for the life of me picture you giving it to him."

Nicole's stomach churned. Her heart seemed to have jumped into her throat, impeding her ability to swallow. *Tell him!* The words burned themselves in her brain. There would never be a better time. She wanted to tell him. All she had to do was to say . . .

"Nicole?" He touched his finger to her cheek and wiped away a tear. "Baby, don't cry."

She was crying? Nicole was astonished. But those were tears gliding silently down her cheeks. Oh God, what was she going to do? She hated the idea of deceiving Drake a moment longer. He'd been so good to her, to her whole family. Didn't she owe him the truth?

Her eyes turned compulsively to Robbie, who was lying on his back, his little fists flung on either side of his head. She stifled a sob. But Robbie was just a baby; his very existence depended on her. Maternal love is a powerful force, and she'd been gifted with an unlimited supply of it. As long as there was even a remote chance that he might be taken from her, she didn't dare risk confessing. Didn't she owe Robbie a future with her?

"Nicole, I'm sorry, honey." Drake pulled her into his arms and rocked her, raining light comforting kisses upon her forehead, her cheeks, the top of her head. "I knew you'd be upset, but I thought you had a right to know."

He'd expected an emotional reaction from her. It couldn't be easy for a woman to learn that she'd been one of three, duped into having a child by the same man.

"I—I'm glad you told me, Drake," she whispered. "After all, those babies are Robbie's sisters!" Her mouth quivered. "Is—is your father going to to—to try to take them away from their mothers?"

Drake laughed harshly. "Oh, honey, there's no danger of that." He told her about Preston's coarse rejection of his grandchildren, whom he'd dismissed as "little bastards." He was ashamed to have to acknowledge his father's heartlessness.

Nicole's tears abruptly ended and her eyes flashed with erupting fury. *Little bastards!* "That's unconscionable, Drake. How dare he talk that way about his own grandchildren!" She disengaged herself from Drake's arms and sat up straight. "Your father owes those children their share of Andrew's estate. The mothers ought to legally demand it."

"I don't disagree, Nicole. But this is Preston Austin we're talking about. He has a whole batallion of lawyers to successfully scare the mothers away. He's practically legally invulnerable."

"I guess appealing to his better nature wouldn't work—the man doesn't have one." Nicole frowned. "And I suppose it stands to reason that any man who was satisfied to let his own son grow up in the same town as his family and not support him is hardly going to be moved by the existence of illegitimate grandchildren."

"Threat of public exposure wouldn't work either," Drake said bitterly. "He always laughed off the gossip about my mother and me. I think he actually relished it. He'd simply make some jokes about Andrew being a chip off the old block and shrug off the scandal. As unfair as the situation is, it's hopeless, Nicole."

"It's not! It can't be! You're still viewing your father through the eyes of a rejected—and awe-struck child, Drake. Things are different now—you're a rich man and you have your own power. You could hire a batallion of lawyers equal to his. Hit your father where it'll really hurt him—in an expensive court fight that he'll ultimately lose!"

Drake stood up. "You're suggesting I take my father to court on behalf of two women who got themselves knocked up by Andrew? For godsakes, Nicole, I can't get involved in something like that."

Nicole scrambled to her feet and grabbed both his wrists with her hands. "You have to, Drake! Think of those babies. Somebody has to help them and why shouldn't it be you? You're their uncle! You're as related to them as you are to Robbie."

"And perhaps you'd like a cut of Andrew's estate for your son?" Drake's lips curled into a sarcastic smile. "I thought you weren't at all interested in Robbie's inheritance, Nicole."

"I'm not. Robbie has me, and I'll always provide for him. But those baby girls . . . if their mothers are anything like Cheryl—and it sounds like they are—they'll need all the help they can get, Drake."

He stared down at her earnest, upturned face, the fervor glowing in her dark blue eyes. And felt suddenly, thoroughly drained. Being around Nicole was akin to riding an emotional roller coaster; it might be exhilarating, but it was also exhausting. She managed to engage him in every way, as no one in the world ever had. The depth and complexity of their relationship took its toll. He felt an inordinate need to withdraw into the undemanding state of indifference.

"If you had their names and addresses, you'd undoubtedly invite them to move in with you," he said wryly.

"I couldn't. I don't have unlimited resources, and I have too many other responsibilities. But you can help them, Drake. You— "

He moved away from her. "Nasty court fights aren't my forte, Nicole. I'm a photographer, remember?" he said lightly. "I look at life through a camera lens. I'm an observer and a recorder, not a crusader like you are."

"Oh, don't fall back on your mellow and laid-back Mr. Cool routine, Drake. It just doesn't work now that I know the *real* you."

He felt his face flush, but managed to inquire coolly, "And who or what might that be, Miss Fortune?"

"A man who gets involved, a compassionate and understanding and generous man who—"

"You're laying it on with a trowel, Nicole. And it's not going to work. *If* I had something to atone for in my relationship with Andrew—and I don't— then taking in you and Robbie, along with the rest of your gang, is my atonement. I won't be railroaded into fighting Preston Austin in court on behalf of two women and their children, none of whom I've ever laid eyes on."

"I'm not talking about some stupid mystical atonement, Drake. I'm talking about two baby girls who are being deprived of what is rightfully theirs, just as you were when you were a child. And by the same man, too."

"You're more relentless than a tornado in full force." Drake made an exclamation of exasperation. "No, Nicole, I won't do it."

She folded her arms in front of her chest and stared intently at him. Undoubtedly gearing up for her next appeal, Drake thought grimly, and decided that Hailey was right about Nicole knowing what to do or say to "make things work out." The way Nicole Fortune wanted them to, he silently added, fighting a grudging admiration for her tenacity. Still, she couldn't win every time. And no matter what she said, he was not going to get involved in this mess. It was strictly between Preston Austin and the young women who claimed to have given birth to Andrew's children.

"Can we drop the subject now?" His tone was challenging. "Or do you want to escalate our differing opinions to a full-fledged quarrel?"

"I told you I hate it when we fight," she said softly. "But this is more than a mere difference of opinion, Drake, it—"

"No." He closed the small distance between them and lightly laid his fingers over her lips. "The subject is closed, unless you want to fight about it." He took her hand and tugged her down to the blanket, where Robbie was still sleeping soundly. "Let's talk about something else."

"Such as?"

"I'd like to take some pictures of you and Robbie—when he's awake, that is. Will you let me?"

She smiled in spite of herself. "Are you kidding? What mother wouldn't jump at the chance to have the great Drake Austin photograph her baby?"

He smiled back at her, and a slow warmth suffused her. No, she definitely didn't want to fight with him. "How did you get started taking pictures, Drake?" she asked, giving in to her insatiable curiosity about him. "When did you decide you wanted to do it full time?"

"I took my first picture when I was thirteen, for the junior high school newspaper. . . ." he began.

They talked about backgrounds and beginnings, likes and dislikes, goals and dreams for the next two hours, until Robbie awakened from his nap, demanding their complete attention.

Late that night, Drake stayed at the house with Nicole and Robbie when the Ruggerios took Hailey and her children to see the fireworks.

"I know a place where we can see the fireworks minus the crowds," Drake said as Nicole joined him downstairs after checking on the sleeping baby. "Want to come with me?" He held out his hand to her.

"You've made me an offer I can't refuse." Nicole slipped her hand in his.

He led her outside to a tall elm tree on the edge of the property. "This is it. You can't beat the view from the top branches."

Nicole eyed the tree dubiously. "You're going to climb it?"

"*We're* going to climb—to the top. I'll help you." He gave her a boost onto a wide branch.

After much laughing and many more boosts and pulls, they made it to a thick, sturdy branch close to the top. "You're the worst tree-climber I've ever met," accused Drake, settling himself on the branch against the trunk of the tree.

"Thanks a lot!" She laughed. "I grew up in the city, remember? I challenge you to find a tree to climb in the middle of Newark, then or now."

"Weak excuse, Nicole. Climbing trees is instinctive."

"Only for those whose near ancestors swung on vines."

"Touché." Grinning, Drake caught her round the middle and pulled her back against him, securing her back to his chest, his hands locked over her stomach.

Nicole leaned against him, her head in the hollow of his shoulder, her hands resting on his arms. The muscles felt strong as steel beneath her fingers. Her legs dangled over the branch, close to his. It was very dark and very quiet at the top of the tree. Very private. Simultaneously, they both sighed. And then laughed self-consciously.

She glanced at the ground, then at the blanket of stars in the night sky above them. "We sure are high," she said on a gulp.

"Relax, I'm not going to let you fall." His breath was warm against her neck and his lips brushed the silky softness of her hair.

Nicole's eyes closed as a sweet prick of desire made her go weak and soft inside. She had already fallen—in love with Drake Austin.

Nine

The hospital in Newark called the next morning with news of Peter's scheduled release. Drake, who'd been looking for an excuse to postpone returning to his apartment in the city, rearranged his schedule and agreed to drive Nicole into Newark and bring Peter back to East Hampton.

During the drive they talked about last night's fireworks display and carried on their mock tree-climbing feud. Drake gleefully reminded Nicole about the difficulty she'd had getting up and down the tree. She attributed his tree-climbing skill to his close simian relatives.

Neither of them mentioned the deep, slow kisses which had transformed last night's two-minute walk back to the house into a twenty-five-minute sensual odyssey. Nor did either mention the restless night each had spent, thinking and longing for the other. But the words hung there, unspoken, yet exchanged with every touch and glance that passed between them.

Peter talked very little on the way back to East Hampton; he seemed anxious and preoccupied. But if his greeting to Nicole and Drake at the hospital had been perfunctory, his whole-hearted smile and hug for Demon was anything but.

"Peter loves that dog so much," Nicole murmured to Drake as they quietly observed the reunion. "Thanks for making it possible for them to be together, Drake."

Drake said nothing. A month ago he would've been aghast at the thought of providing a home for a convalescing mental patient and a dog who was almost the size of a sports car. Now he felt glad he'd been able to do it. Not resigned or indifferent. Glad! It was a peculiar moment of enlightenment.

The two of them watched Peter put on headphones which were plugged into his Walkman and sit in a rocking chair on the back porch. He began to rock, staring out at the sea. Demon flopped loyally alongside him.

"At least Peter's getting some fresh air," Nicole said to Drake from their vantage point inside the kitchen. "Back home in Newark, he sat under the air conditioner in the hall all day."

"Doesn't he even watch TV?" asked Drake.

"Incessantly at times. And at other times it disturbs him—he thinks the people in it are talking to him. He loves to listen to tapes with the headphones on, though. He says it drowns out the voices he hears in his head."

Drake shook his head. "It seems like such a waste, having him just sit around all the time by himself. Isn't there some kind of program . . ."

"There's nothing. There's no funding for community mental health centers for patients like Peter to go to. Ideally, he should be in a residential treatment home. I found a wonderful one, Glenview Acres, in Pennsylvania, where the patients live in small family-type groups in cottages. Pets are allowed, so Demon could stay with him. They have all kinds of recreational activities and vocational training in lots of different areas. He would be with people his own age and trained counselors. . . ." She sighed. "It would be just perfect for him."

"So why doesn't he go there?"

"That old bugaboo, money." Nicole grimaced. "The annual cost for a patient to live there is slightly less than my annual salary as a teacher. And they don't take anybody who can't pay. They don't have to. Since it's such an excellent facility, they have no trouble filling it."

She gazed out at Peter, her blue eyes troubled. "I know I'm not doing enough for Peter and I—"

"You're doing the best you can, Nicole," Drake interrupted. He cupped her shoulders with his hands and began a gentle massage. "You're doing more than anyone else is doing for him. Including his own family, wherever they may be."

She turned in his arms and they kissed, tenderly at first and then with rising passion. Nicole moaned softly as Drake's tongue rubbed hers and began an erotic duel that sent blazing flames of desire streaking through her.

All too soon he was lifting his head. She pressed her forehead against his chest and clung to him, reluctant to leave his arms. Every time they kissed, it grew harder to let him go.

"Let's take a walk into the village," he said huskily, taking her hand. "There are too many people around here for me to do what I really want to do with you."

"And that is?" she drawled, gazing seductively at him through lowered lashes.

"Carry you up to bed—as if you didn't know." He strode from the house, dragging her along with him. Laughing, she had to almost run to keep up with him.

They strolled along Main Street, lined on both sides with huge elm trees, and wandered in and out of the small shops. They walked around the pond in the village green and gazed at the artists exhibiting their wares. It was a pleasant, companionable afternoon which neither wanted to end.

The next two weeks were equally idyllic. Drake phoned Carmen in the city and told her to reschedule all his appointments. For the first time in his life, he found something he wanted to do more than to take pictures. For the first time there was a rival for his previously all-consuming passion for photography. Her name was Nicole Fortune.

They were together constantly. The two of them spent hours taking long walks and having long talks. There was kissing and laughing, playing with Robbie and Hailey's children, boat rides for two in Drake's sleek cigarette boat and family rides in the larger cabin cruiser. They swam and sunned themselves, cooked picnic dinners on the outdoor grill, and walked the kids into town for ice cream.

Drake took Nicole and Peter sailing several times, and Nicole seemed delighted that Peter turned out to be a better sailor than she. She praised and encouraged him. There was none of the competition and one-upmanship that festered among the Austin siblings, Drake noted. He admired Nicole's loyalty and confidence. She didn't need to build herself up at the expense of another.

Something he'd been doing all his life, Drake realized with a shock of self-awareness. He'd continually compared himself to Andrew—and to a lesser extent, the two younger Austins—and felt reaffirmed each time they failed where he'd succeeded. It was a sobering realization. He'd always placed the blame for their hostile relationship on his father and brothers. For the first time, he considered that he hadn't been quite as righteous as he'd always thought.

And with that acknowledgment came a faint hope that maybe things could be different between him and his brothers. Andrew was gone, but it might not be too late to alter his relationship with Dane and Ian. Nicole was right, he wasn't as indifferent as he pretended to be. He had a strong sense of family that he'd been suppressing for years, behind his cool facade. He made a decision to take the first step to try to reach some level of understanding with his surviving half brothers.

He credited Nicole with his newfound insights. She held nothing back with those she loved. Being around her was a living lesson in familial love and loyalty. But there was a down side to spending so much time with her as well: frustration to the point of madness when it came to sex.

Never had he wanted a woman more. Never had he felt this overpowering *need* for a woman. And not just any woman. It would be so simple if all he wanted was to get laid, Drake thought ruefully. There were any number of names in his little black book that he could call for a no-strings roll in the sack. But he wanted Nicole Fortune; no one else would do.

And she was holding back. Though he knew she wanted him, night after night she sent him to his bedroom alone. The strain of wanting and not having was beginning to take its toll. He'd never felt so powerfully and totally involved or so intense in his life.

"Are you playing games with me?" Drake asked one sultry night as Nicole pulled out of his arms after countless long, torrid kisses. "Everybody is in bed, asleep. Why won't you come to my room and make love with me? You know you want to— and you know how much I want you to."

"Yes," she whispered achingly. Each night it grew harder to stop the kisses and caresses and go to her room alone. She loved Drake; he was the only man she would ever love, she was certain of that. How long could she go on fighting her own passionate longing plus her strong need to please him? She wanted nothing to stand between them; there must be no more secrets, either emotional or sexual.

Her eyes glowed with love. And with purpose. Tonight she would prove her love in the most elemental and profound way. It was time. But there were things she needed to tell him first— and she would tell him everything.

"Oh, Drake, I want you so much, but I—"

"No more buts," Drake said forcefully. The love light in her eyes inspired him. It told him exactly what he needed to know. "No more reasons why or why not." Words were unnecessary. She wanted him to take her, wanted him to take charge. "I should have done this in the beginning and saved us both a lot of sleepless nights." He scooped her up into his arms and captured her mouth with his, his lips warm and hard and insistent.

The fireworks inside her head rivaled the spectacular Independence Day display. Nicole clung to Drake, meeting the demands of his lips and his tongue, and making equally sensuous demands of her own.

Her senses were spinning as his mouth left hers to nibble on the curve of her neck as he carried her up the stairs and down the hall. "I want you more than I've ever wanted any woman, Nicole," he muttered in a sexy growl that sent exciting shivers tingling along her spine. And then they were in his room. He paused for a few seconds to close and lock the door behind them.

It was dark in the bedroom. The light from the downstairs hall crept in around the cracks, providing only a faint, shadowy illumination. Drake set Nicole on her feet, letting her body slide slowly along the length of him, turning her release into a long, intimate caress in itself.

Nicole's knees trembled and came dangerously close to buckling under her. She clutched at the front of his shirt to support herself, lifting her eyes to focus on the full, sensual line of his mouth. She knew he could read her every emotion in her eyes, but she had no thoughts of concealing them. She wanted no secrets between them anymore. Her love, her passion for him was honest and real and nothing to hide.

His arms came around her, and Nicole felt the male strength in them. He made her feel gloriously feminine, small and fragile and cherished. She breathed in his familiar masculine scent and a delicious heat flowed through her. She drew a deep, shaky breath, wanting to feel his mouth on hers again with an intensity so fierce that it bordered on pain.

"Oh God, Nicole," he murmured thickly, his eyes affixed to her face as his hands closed possessively over the swollen softness of her breasts. He flicked his thumbs over the taut peaks which were achingly sensitive, even through the layers of her clothing.

Nicole uttered a strangled little cry as he thrust his thigh between hers. The pressure there was an exquisite pleasure and she strained closer, wanting more. Hot, honeyed flames burned through her, spreading through her body like liquid fire.

"Nicole, I have to have you." Drake's voice was gruff with need. He glided his hands over her, feeling her, learning her body. He smoothed his palms over the firm flatness of her belly, over the gentle slope of her hips before his hands closed heavily over her derriere. He fitted her into the hard heat of his thighs, letting her feel the full force of his burgeoning strength.

He gazed down at her. Her eyes were closed, her cheeks flushed, her lips parted and slightly swollen from his kisses. She was the image of a woman melting into passion, trusting and open and so intensely vulnerable. She was passionate and aroused, surrendering herself so completely, so lovingly to him.

She felt his fingers on the zipper of her sundress. With a deft movement, he swept the dress from her, letting it drop into a pale pink pool at her feet. Standing before him in her lacy pink bra and matching bikini panties, Nicole began to lose her nerve.

Sensing her sudden apprehension, Drake drew her into his arms and kissed her tenderly, lingeringly. "I don't ever want you to feel shy with me, Nicole," he murmured softly. "You're so sexy and sweet." He unclasped the front fastener of her bra and slipped it from her shoulders. "And so very beautiful." He cupped her breasts in his hands and squeezed gently, erotically.

She shivered as a wave of delicious weakness spun through her. "Oh, Drake!" His name was a yearning cry of passion and need. The voluptuous emotions pulsing through her were dizzying. But the most powerful, overriding one was love.

Slowly, carefully, he eased her down onto the bed, leaving her for just a moment to flick on the bedside lamp. "I want to be able to see you," he explained huskily.

"Drake, no!" she protested. Her whole body was one heated blush. "Please, I—I like it better off."

He smiled at her. "You're much too beautiful and much too desirable for an anonymous grope in the dark." He gazed down at her breasts with dark, hungry eyes, then began to circle her nipples with his fingers, moving them up and down and around until the taut pink tips were swollen into hard little points.

Nicole's breathing grew heavy. Her eyelids fluttered shut and she moaned with pure sensual need.

"You're very sensitive there," Drake observed with a sexy smile. He touched his lips to her neck and kissed a sensuous trail from her throat to her throbbing nipples which were thrusting against his hands.

His mouth closed hotly over one rigid crest, and Nicole thought she might faint from the breath-takingly intense pleasure. She whimpered his name and clasped his head to her breast. He used his tongue and his teeth and his lips on first one breast and then the other, wringing soft, deep cries from her as she writhed in fervent abandon.

"Oh, Drake, it feels so good," she whispered on a breathy sigh.

Her sexual openness and honesty inflamed him further. "Sweet Nicole," he rasped urgently. "You're so responsive, so passionate."

Knowing that she pleased him excited her almost as much as his touch. She ran her fingers convulsively through the dark thickness of his hair. "Drake," she whispered. "I feel like I'm *burning* for you."

"Good," he rasped. Her artless and heartfelt cry was almost unbearably exciting. She made him feel like the most powerful lover in the world. "I want you to burn for me, baby."

She gazed up at him, her face flushed with passion and radiant with love. It was an irresist-ible combination. Drake felt as if Roman candles were exploding in his head. He hated to let her go, even for the few moments it took to shed his clothes.

He came back to her nude, and Nicole's fingers tangled in the soft mat of dark hair on his chest, thrilling to the bare warmth of his body. She ran her hands over the solid muscles of his shoulders, over the long, smooth length of his back, intoxi-cated by the exciting masculine feel of him. She felt him shudder with response under her hands and knew the heady thrill of her own feminine power.

Daringly, she inched her hands lower to the taut, bare curve of his buttocks. When his body clenched in a sudden spasm, she quickly drew back. He was splendidly, fully aroused. She stared at him. "Oh, Drake," she sighed. "I love looking at you almost as much as I love touching you."

Once more, her breathless candor nearly drove him over the edge. "Nicole, what you do to me . . ." His voice trailed off. He couldn't talk, couldn't think. His whole body was pounding, so hot he felt he would explode any minute.

He pulled her against him, his hands pressing her tightly up and into him, his mouth greedily fierce on hers. His fingers traced the silky outline of her panties, then delved beneath the lace-trimmed edges, skimming the hot, smooth skin beneath.

Nicole was lost in an erotic dream. She clung to Drake, glorying in the feel of his hard, hot mouth slanted over hers, of his tongue deep in her mouth. The wiry hair on his chest was sensuously abrasive to her sensitized nipples and she rubbed her breasts against him, shivering at the titillating friction her movements elicited.

And then his big, warm hand slid inside her panties and Nicole gasped at the unfamiliar intimacy. She felt his fingers glide through the dark soft down that guarded her feminine secrets. She was swollen and flowing, and his shocking, sensual caresses sent her spinning into an all new dimension of rapture.

Pleasure built and grew within her and she trembled at the thrilling sensations his clever hands aroused. When he took off her panties, she moaned and shifted her legs, opening herself to his touch, moving her hips sinuously in wordless invitation.

He caressed her with tantalizing fingers, stroking and parting the vulnerable softness of her, applying an exquisite pressure which gave her such ecstasy she wanted to scream with it.

And then she was crying aloud because the spiral of pleasure had gathered force and tightened to the breaking point. Her body exploded in a shattering firestorm as waves of pleasure poured through her. She arched like a drawn bow as a succession of rapturous paroxysms rocked her body. And then she went limp, a warm, glowing warmth radiating throughout her entire body.

Slowly, she opened her eyes to find Drake gazing down at her, his expression intent, his blue eyes glimmering with sensuality. She blushed and swiftly averted her eyes, then rolled on her side away from him.

Drake was baffled by her reaction. Observing her unconditional response to him had been incredibly exciting and arousing. He'd watched her face as ecstasy rippled through her and felt a vicarious satisfaction, knowing that he was the man to give her such pleasure. But now . . .

She wouldn't look at him. She had turned her back on him, literally. Was she angry? he wondered uneasily. Could this be some kind of new female torture she'd dreamed up to drive him crazy? He couldn't tolerate the thought. A rush of sheer masculine fury coursed through him.

"Nicole!" He pulled her around to face him. Cupping her chin, he forced her to meet his eyes. "Look at me."

Nicole thought of the way she had been, writhing and moaning and completely out of control. *And he had been watching her!* The realization totally unnerved her. She closed her eyes and went hot all over again. "Oh, Drake, I don't know what to say. I—I've—That's never happened to me before," she said haltingly. She clamped her teeth over her lower lip and tried to breathe deeply to regain her control.

Drake stared at her. "You're *embarrassed?*" he managed to ask at last.

She nodded weakly.

"You're embarrassed because you climaxed?" he pressed, trying to get it straight.

She winced and lowered her eyes.

Drake's anger faded as quickly as it had come. The full significance of her words sent him reeling. "You mean I'm the first man to make you come?" Already swollen with desire, he now swelled with pure male pride.

Nicole managed a wavering smile, but she felt more like crying. She remembered that she'd wanted to tell him everything before they were intimate and knew that her instincts had been correct. Informing him of her virginity at this particular point was clearly dreadful timing.

She stroked his cheek with trembling fingertips. "You're the first man, Drake," she blurted out. "Period."

It took several seconds for her words to sink in. And even then, they didn't. Not really. "I'm not sure I understand," he said cautiously.

She drew a deep breath. There was no other way to tell him than to simply come right out and say it. "I'm a virgin, Drake."

His eyes grew hard. "You have a child, Nicole. Or have you somehow forgotten giving birth to Robbie—and conceiving him in Andrew's bed?"

Nicole couldn't look at him. "I never knew your half brother and I didn't give birth to Robbie," she said, the blood roaring in her ears. "M-My foster sister Cheryl Graham did. Andrew, uh, approached her and . . . and the result was Robbie. He said he was Drake Austin and that's the name that Cheryl put on Robbie's birth certificate. She knew she couldn't take care of a baby at this point in her life so she gave him to me when he was born. I . . . I'm going to legally adopt him." Whenever there was some extra money to pay the necessary legal fees.

But she didn't bother to add that fact; not with the cold accusing look on his face. If she mentioned the word *money*, he would probably accuse her of trying to weasel it from him. A chill ran through her. Suppose he were to think that anyway? He'd already accused her of it once before.

Drake abruptly stood up. Her words were ringing in his ears. Disbelief turned to incredulity and then quickly to fury. *She was a virgin? She'd never even known Andrew, let alone slept with him? She wasn't Robbie's mother. She had lied to him. All this time, she'd been lying!*

"You conniving little bitch!" His voice shook with the force of his emotions. He glared down at her as she huddled, naked and miserable, on the bed. "What kind of a double-crossing scheme are you trying to pull off?"

She flinched. "There is no scheme, Drake. I am Robbie's mother in every way that counts. I have been since I took him home from the hospital, when he was just three days old and—"

"Shut up!" Drake thundered. "I don't want to hear any more of your lies."

"I'm not a liar." Her voice rose. "I only let you believe that I'd given birth to Robbie because I was afraid that you might—that you would—try to take him away from me."

Drake's eyes narrowed. "Why would I do that?" he snapped.

His face was a mask of fury. Nicole quivered. "Because you're his blood relative. Legally, you—you have a bona fide family tie to him."

"And you think I'd tear a baby from the arms of the only mother he's ever known? What kind of a monster do you think I am, Nicole?"

"I don't think you're a monster at all! But I know you now and I didn't know you that day I walked into your office." Her voice cracked. It was so hard to sit here, acting so sane and civilized when some wild part of her wanted to scream with pain.

"Walked into my office demanding money!" Drake amended acidly.

"I thought you were his father, remember? That's the name Andrew gave to Cheryl." And to the two other gullible young women who'd had babies by him, though she refrained from adding it. Things were already bad enough.

"Cheryl." His mouth tautened to a thin line. "Another one of Andrew's empty-headed bimbos. Damn, it all makes sense now. I knew you and Andrew wouldn't make it through two minutes of conversation, much less to the bedroom! Yet all this time, you've been deceiving me. . . ." His voice trailed off. He'd been tortured by images of her and Andrew, and nothing had happened between them. Nothing had happened between her and any man. She was a virgin. Or so she claimed.

"And now this virgin tale . . ." He glowered at her, the anger flowing through his veins like an infusion of an intravenous drug. "You don't actually expect me to believe that a hot little number like you has never been with a man?" His laugh was harsh and hurtful. "What other stories are you going to spin in your relentless quest for cash?"

"I'm not after your money," she cried, her blue eyes filling with tears. She stood up quickly and began to gather her clothes. Her whole body was one hot blush and she was terribly ashamed of her nakedness. What had been beautiful and loving between them now seemed ugly and cheap. "Oh, what's the use trying to explain. You don't want to even try to understand, you *want* to condemn me."

She hurried quickly toward the bathroom, her

clothes in her arms. Drake stood up and followed her. "Come back here!" he bellowed. "I'm not through with you yet."

She fought the overwhelming urge to burst into tears. No, she wouldn't cry even if it meant holding her breath to hold back the tears. Drake would accuse her of using tears to manipulate him. Keeping her face a rigid, poker-straight mask, she rushed to the bathroom and locked the door. She sank down onto the rim of the tub and buried her face in her hands. Her stomach was roiling and she felt like throwing up.

She'd closed the door in his face! Drake stared at the white-painted wood of the door. If he'd been just another centimeter or two closer, it would've hit him smack on the nose. Furiously, he turned the doorknob. It was locked and he twisted it again. "Open the door, Nicole. I want to talk to you."

There was silence on the other side of the door and the lock remained secure. A mixture of impatience and ire began to build within him. "Nicole!" His voice rose. "Let me in!" Still there was no response. "Nicole, if you don't unlock the door this minute, I'm going to kick it in."

The door opened and Nicole stood before him, fully dressed. Her taut composure was in dramatic contrast to his frenzied agitation. She was dressed and controlled; he was nude and aroused, sexually, physically, emotionally. In any sort of confrontation, he would clearly emerge the loser and Drake knew it. The acknowledgment was the emotional equivalent of pouring gasoline on an open fire. She tried to step around him, but he planted himself in front of her, blocking her way.

"Drake, let's not drag this out," Nicole pleaded. "I know you hate me and I'll—"

"That's right. I hate you!" he interrupted, his blue eyes wild. "You're the first woman who's ever made a fool of me and you did a world-class job of it. All the time we've spent together . . . I let you get closer to me than anyone. . . . And you couldn't be bothered to tell me the truth. . . ."

"Drake, I wanted to!" His incoherent fury was breaking her heart. She'd hurt him. She'd never thought he would be hurt by her evasion. Infuriated, perhaps, even vengeful. Too late she realized how he viewed her behavior. He'd let her get close to him, he'd trusted her, and now he thought she'd been using him in a planned charade. She wanted to cry at the betrayal he must be feeling. "At first I was afraid to tell you and then I didn't know how to do it," she cried. "But I was going to tell you tonight. I wanted you to know everything before we—"

"You were going to tell me tonight?" He laughed coldly. "Now why don't I believe that, Nicole?"

She swallowed. "Drake, is what I've done so awful? So unforgivable? I wanted to protect Robbie. He's just a little boy and I'm all he's got. I had to be sure that—"

"I was crazy about you?" Drake supplied caustically. "That you had me wrapped so firmly around your little finger that you could say or do anything and I'd smile like a sap and give you whatever you want?" The fact that he'd come so very close to that very state further inflamed him. "You're a clever little hustler, Nicole, but the game's over. So spare me your heartrending maternal spiel."

Her lips quivered, but she held her head high. "I'm willing to accept responsibility for my actions and admit that what I did was wrong," she said quietly. "I'll say I'm sorry for hurting you, and lying to you, too. I *am* sorry. But what I won't do is to stand here any longer and let you verbally abuse me. I'm not a hot little number or a liar or a hustler or a conniving schemer out to rob you of your precious money and I won't listen to you say that I am."

He planted his hands on either side of the door jamb, effectively surrounding her. "You never know when to quit, do you, Nicole? You're in a very precarious position, baby. I'd advise you to drop the air of injured pride and try to placate me. Keep in mind that I could throw you and your whole family out of my house this minute and you'd all have to go. And I could keep Robbie, *my nephew*, with me and—"

"Stop threatening me." Impulsively, Nicole gave him a shove. It was so strong and unexpected that she succeeded in knocking him aside. She strode past him, her blue eye glittering with rage. "I've never given in to threats and the bullies who make them, and I'm not about to start now. If you want us out of your house, that's your prerogative, but we'll leave in the morning, not in the middle of the night. And Robbie goes with me."

She strode toward the door without looking back. Which was a tactical error because she didn't see him spring to action and follow her. She didn't realize how close he was to her until he grabbed her arm and swung her around to face him.

"No one is going anywhere, Nicole. Particularly not you. Not now. We have some unfinished business between us." His voice lowered and his tone was all silky, sexy menace. He yanked her closer.

Nicole became heart-stoppingly aware of his nudity. Involuntarily, her eyes flicked down his front and hot color scalded her cheeks. When she lifted her eyes she saw him watching her intently. Her heart slammed against her ribcage and began to beat at double time.

"As you can see, I still want you," Drake rasped, taking her hand and guiding it to the undisputable evidence of his need. When her slim fingers tentatively, shakily curved around him, he drew in a painful, ragged breath. "I don't want to want you but I do. I hate you but I want you, want you. . . ." His voice trailed off and he made a sound that was an indistinct combination of a groan and a moan, of pain and pleasure.

And quite suddenly Nicole's anger dissolved and her heart blazed with love for him. He was hurt. He felt betrayed. By her. And the depth of his pain and betrayal could only mean that he cared for her. More than she'd dared to hope. More than he wanted to admit. Her hand held him tightly, and guided by pure sensual instinct, she began a rhythmic milking motion.

Drake immediately thrust her away from him. "Get out of here, Nicole," he said, his voice deep and thick. "Before I—"

"I love you, Drake." She stared into his eyes, her blue eyes dilated and intense. "And I want you so much. Please . . . don't send me away."

"Nicole!" The modicum of control he'd managed to maintain snapped and his arms encircled her and he crushed her against him. "No, baby, I won't send you away. I can't do it. I can't let you go."

Between wild kisses, they stumbled back to the bed. Drake stripped her of her clothes, and this time he wasn't deft and smooth. His movements were heavy, his fingers awkward and thick. All of his sensual coordination seemed to have vanished in the dizziness of wild desire.

He came down on top of her and Nicole clung to him, holding him tight, moving her body beneath him, glorying in the feel of their naked flesh pressed tightly together. She needed to feel his weight upon her, needed his mouth hot and hard on hers, needed . . . something she had never known and couldn't describe. But she ached. And her body yearned.

She felt his throbbing masculine strength thrusting against her and she melted like hot honey. It felt so wonderful, so right for the two of them to be lying here together, kissing, loving, learning, and sharing their bodies' most intimate secrets. *At last.* She didn't care about their shattering quarrel. All that mattered was that she loved Drake and they were finally together like this.

She was so glad that she'd waited all these years for Drake, her first lover, Nicole thought dazedly. She'd scorned herself for being a repressed romantic, but this moment made up for all the time spent dreaming. It had been a long, lonely wait, but now she was finally with the man she'd been born to love.

She watched him reach inside the drawer of the bedside stand and remove a foil-wrapped condom. And she loved him even more for the care he was taking of her. He was thoughtful and dependable and reliable, a man who could be counted on.

They lay together on the bed, kissing, petting, soft moans and sensual sighs breaking the intimate late night silence of the room.

"Tell me what to do, Drake," she breathed. "I want to please you. I want to give you everything you want. . . ."

He was half out of his head, and her words, so soft and promising and excruciatingly sexy, caused him to become totally unglued. He couldn't talk, he couldn't think. He could only react and he did, possessively, hungrily. Holding her hips, he drove himself into her, moaning deeply when her body closed tightly and hotly around him.

Nicole tensed at the sudden stab of pain and she felt a convulsive tremor rack his body.

"Are you all right?" Drake asked hoarsely. "Am I hurting you?" He forced himself to lie still within her until her body adjusted to the impact of his.

She felt him inside her, filling her, making her melt and flow in the most thrilling way. And then he began to move, slowly at first. Nicole trembled as hot waves of pleasure washed over her. His strokes grew deeper and longer and quickened in pace. She arched and moaned and clung to him, matching her movements to his, complementing his masculine rhythm with her own feminine motion.

His desire spurred hers and hers incited his, higher and higher, until they were soaring into a fiery stratosphere of rapture. And then a cataclysmic burst of pleasure hurled them into a sensual whirlwind and together they rode the storm to a shimmering, mind-shattering release.

Nicole shivered under the sheet and groped for the blanket at the foot of the bed. The ceiling fan enhanced the cooling effects of the stiff breeze which was blowing the curtains away from the window.

Just a short while ago she had been warm, her body glowing with a sweet, sensual languor as Drake lay on top of her and inside her, both of them replete from the explosive climax of their passion. And then, abruptly, jarringly, he had left her.

It had happened so fast she hadn't had time to protest. Drake withdrew from her physically and then strode from the room, not looking back, not saying a word. He hadn't come back, and now she lay alone and shivering in his bed, trying to hold back the tears which threatened.

She loved him; their lovemaking was everything she'd ever dreamed about and more. She had been sure that in its aftermath they would be closer than ever.

Obviously, she was wrong. Drake had said he hated her and she had to face the fact that perhaps he hadn't been merely caught up in the volatility of the moment, as she'd thought. *As she'd hoped*, she corrected herself miserably. Maybe he actually meant it. Her heart froze and she forced herself to consider it. Drake hated her. It was all over between them and he wanted her out of his life. He couldn't even stand to stay in the same room—or the same bed!—with her, so great was his aversion to her.

Nicole felt hot tears stream down her cheeks and she made no effort to check them. The morning would come soon enough and she would have to face the others and be strong. Tonight she could let herself be weak. Alone in the darkness, she didn't have to conceal her heartbreak from anybody.

She cried for a long, long time before she fell into a restless sleep.

Ten

Nicole awakened the next morning with a pounding headache, a churning stomach, and a heavy heart. She crept from Drake's bedroom to her own and swiftly showered and dressed, but her morning ablutions made her feel no better. She wore her black shorts and black T-shirt without the hot pink belt that usually gave the outfit a splash of color. Today there was no color in her world. She felt as if she were in mourning and dressed to suit her dark emotions.

She carried Robbie to the kitchen to give him his breakfast, and every time she heard a noise she jumped, thinking it was Drake. She dreaded seeing him. The prospect of his treating her coldly—and he would—brought a fresh wave of tears to her eyes.

Which she forced herself not to shed. Today was going to be terrible enough for her family without them having to observe the unheard-of spectacle of Nicole crying. As she spoon-fed Robbie his oatmeal, and sliced pieces of banana which he fed himself with his fingers, she rehearsed how she would tell Hailey and Peter that they were leaving today. It would be just as hard taking Johnny,

Julie, and Jeffrey away, too. They were so happy here. It was a paradise of a home for them all.

Berating herself for her cowardice, she postponed breaking the bad news all during breakfast. And then Hailey took her kids out to the pool—they loved the water so much, Drake said that all three were natural-born swimmers and had mentioned swimming lessons for them—and Nicole decided that they might as well have one last peaceful swim.

Peter took Demon for a walk along the shore, his expression less wooden, his movements less mechanical than usual. He'd made a relatively easy adjustment to life here. It would be a different story when they returned to Newark and whatever temporary housing was available. Somehow they would have to find a way to keep the dog with them, she thought anxiously. She couldn't put Peter through another separation from his beloved pet.

Finally, she grew tired of tensing every time she heard a sound and asked Rich Ruggerio where Drake was. Rich, his easel and paints under his arm, told her that Drake had left shortly after dawn to shoot a sunglasses ad further down the beach.

"A whole crew arrived. I'm surprised you didn't hear them," said Rich, frowning. "They made enough noise to wake the dead. And then Drake wanted Linda to make coffee for the whole group. At that hour! Can you imagine?"

Nicole's lips twitched. Despite her misery, she saw the humor in Rich's indignation. For a moment she forgot that Drake detested her and planned to share the joke of his daring to ask his housekeeper to make coffee for his guests! But the leaden feeling in her chest reminded her that there would be no more shared jokes with Drake. No more laughter, no more long talks, no more kisses. It was all over between them. He'd made love to her, wanting her sexually but despising her. Pain sliced through her, as sharp as a stiletto.

She swallowed around the huge lump that had lodged in her throat. Drake hadn't mentioned that he was working this morning. She knew he'd done some rearranging of his schedule to spend time out here with them these past few weeks. Now it appeared that it was business as usual again. Did that mean he wanted the Fortune clan out before he returned?

Rich and Linda went out to paint, and Nicole procrastinated some more, avoiding the arduous job of packing their things by playing with Robbie. They were in the midst of a rousing game of peek-a-boo when the door chimes sounded. She carried the baby to the door to answer it.

Her jaw dropped comically agape when she saw who was standing on the porch, waiting to be admitted into the house. "Thad Griffin?" she gasped incredulously.

The man, wearing pale yellow slacks and a pea-cock-blue T-shirt with an oversized pastel jacket, removed his mirrored sunglasses and smiled. "That's right." He seemed pleased that she'd recognized him. "And you are?"

"P-Pleased to meet you," Nicole stammered and then realized that he'd expected her to give him her name. She forced herself to close her mouth, but she couldn't stop staring. Thad Griffin defined tall, dark, and handsome. She'd seen him in the movies, larger than life, when he'd been an actor, and then thrilled to the Academy Award-winning films he'd directed. The small lines around his eyes and the silver tips which lightened the ends of his glossy black hair were indicative of his forty years, yet didn't detract at all from his devastating masculine appeal.

Robbie threw his blue plastic teething pretzel on the floor and called out, "Uh-oh," with proud delight. Thad smilingly bent to hand the baby the toy and Nicole was on the verge of smiling back and thanking him when it hit her. Thad Griffin had cast Robbie's birth mother in a porn film! Only Drake's intervention had spared Cheryl from the degradation and humiliation her appearance in such a film would have entailed.

Nicole took several steps back, her blue eyes turning icy. "Drake isn't here right now," she said, fixing him with a disapproving glare. "I'd invite you in but I can't stomach the thought of being under the same roof as the man who wanted to—to debase my little sister!"

Griffin seemed to pale under his tan. "Then you're—you're—" He stared at Robbie. "And you and Drake have a baby? Oh God!" He was perspiring now and pulled out a spotless white handkerchief to wipe his brow. "I swear I didn't know that Cheryl Graham was your sister or I never would've—"

Nicole closed the door in midsentence and started to walk away. She was shaking with anger. As if today weren't bad enough, that monster Griffin had to show up! She wondered why he was here and decided she didn't care. Maybe there was one very thin silver lining in the cloud hanging over her life. If Drake had decided to renew his friendship with Thad Griffin, at least she wouldn't be around to watch.

Griffin knocked on the door and rang the chimes again. And again. "Please, Nicole," he called through the closed door. "I want to apologize. And to reassure you that when Drake called we hadn't shot a single frame of—er—objectionable footage."

Furiously, Nicole flung open the door. "Objectionable footage!" she howled. "Skip the euphemisms, you creep! Raunchy X-rated sleaze by any other name is still raunchy X-rated sleaze. And you cast my sister in it!"

Griffin wiped his face again. His color was almost ashen. "Nicole, I'm sorry. I honestly didn't know that Cheryl's sister was Drake Austin's girlfriend. God, and you're the mother of his child, too! Things can't get any worse!"

He began to pace the porch, wringing his hands. "My life has been collapsing around me lately. Everything seems to be falling apart. It's as if I'm living under some kind of curse or something. First I got a surprise audit from the IRS and they unearthed some tax breaks my accountants used a few years back. Next thing I know I'm facing charges of income tax evasion and a suit for three million dollars in back taxes. Then immigration came snooping around and charged me with hiring illegal aliens as my housekeeping staff. Hell, everybody does it in LA and have been doing it for years, but they threw the book at me. And then, the same day Drake called to tell me I'd hired his lover's sister to star in a piece of trash guaranteed to bring in some quick money to pay my lawyers, the police department phoned to inform me that I have eight thousand dollars of unpaid parking tickets and am facing jail. Jail, for not paying a few damn parking tickets!"

"Eight thousand dollars' worth is more than a few. I hope you do go to jail." Nicole glowered at him. "You deserve to, and for more than the parking tickets."

"You obviously haven't forgiven me." Griffin looked distraught. "Does that mean that Drake hasn't either? I can't afford to lose his goodwill—he's too influential in too many circles. I can't afford to lose anyone's goodwill these days. I have to try to redeem myself. That's why I'm here, to set things to right in person, Nicole. I'm throwing myself on your mercy. Please forgive me. Don't let Drake blackball me among—"

"How do you know my name?" Nicole interrupted curiously, her anger abating somewhat. The man seemed close to hysteria. She wondered if he was on the verge of some kind of nervous breakdown.

"Drake told me, of course. And when I asked Cheryl about you she told me how protective you've always been of her. How you once knocked out the front teeth of a boy who tried to manhandle her." He gave his head a rueful shake. "I swear that we hadn't started shooting the—er—pornographic scenes, Nicole. There were a few nude scenes filmed but I personally destroyed them."

Drake had told Thad Griffin she was his girlfriend, exactly what he'd said he wouldn't say, Nicole mused. But that was before he'd learned of her deception, and it was irrelevant now. Drake hated her. He'd told her so and then left her in disgust. Pain shadowed her face.

Griffin, taking encouragement from the fact that she hadn't condemned him again or wished him in jail, continued hopefully, "I made sure Cheryl got her job back in the jewelry boutique and I paid the next three months' rent on her apartment for her. Have you heard from her since she's been back in Florida?"

Nicole nodded. "She called a few days ago. She doesn't seem at all affected by her experience with you—thank heavens! She was a little disappointed that you decided not to make the 'art film' after all, but she likes Florida and she has a new boyfriend. He's a sixty-seven-year-old widower who's a retired diamond merchant. Compared to Cheryl's usual choice of man, he sounds downright wholesome."

Thad Griffin smiled hesitantly. "You're not at all like Cheryl, you know. And I can see why Drake is in love with you. If you were free, I'd—"

"It just so happens I am free," she interjected sarcastically. "I'm leaving here today with my baby and the rest of my family. So if you really want to get on Drake's good side, you'll spare him the time and trouble of having to move us, and do it for him."

"Hell, you mean I walked into the middle of a

big breakup scene?" Griffin looked annoyed. "My abysmal luck just never quits!"

"Go rent a van," Nicole ordered. "Then you can drive my family and me back to Newark. It's your big chance, Griffin. Drake will be indebted to you forever for—"

"Sparing him a drive to Newark," muttered Griffin. "Oh, hell, I suppose you're right. What choice do I have? I'm up to my neck in enemies. If I could do a favor for Drake Austin . . ."

"Situation ethics," Nicole said dryly. "That's probably why you're in trouble with everybody, Griffin. If you leave now to get the van we'll be able to—"

She halted at the sound of the car engine. She and Griffin turned to see two cars and a Jeep pull into the driveway. Nicole froze as Drake bounded out of his red Ferrari Testarossa. He was wearing cut-off jeans and a tank top that emphasized his bronze skin and muscular frame. Tears filled her eyes at the sight of him. She loved him so much and she had to leave him. The rest of her life loomed before her, all the long and lonely years without him.

"Are you okay?" Griffin murmured under his breath. "You look like you're going to faint."

She didn't trust herself to answer. She wished she could faint and gain at least a few moments of relief from the pain that was lacerating her heart. But she didn't faint and the pain grew worse, for Drake was lifting a beautiful young woman, dressed in a short, frilly white dress and sandals, from the passenger side of the car. The girl linked her arms around his neck and laughed up into his eyes as he began to carry her to the house. Her long, dark hair hung over his arm like a luxuriant silk curtain.

A gasp sounded and for a moment, Nicole thought it had come from her. But no, her throat muscles, like the rest of her, were too paralyzed with shock and pain for her to make any sounds or movements. It was Thad Griffin who had gasped. He was staring at Drake and the beautiful young woman in his arms.

'I can't believe this!" Griffin croaked. "Of all the women in the world, why does it have to be *her*?"

"Who is she?" Nicole asked numbly.

"Angelynne Flynn. She's done some modeling, some commercials. She's on some idiotic soap opera—"

"She plays Kimberly!" Nicole nodded her head in recognition. "Peter watches that show sometimes. He always worries about Kimberly and tries to warn her because she's forever in danger."

"She's wasting her talent," Griffin muttered. "She could be an important film star if—"

"In your creepy porn flick?" Nicole scowled. And then her gaze returned compulsively to Drake and Angelynne, who were drawing nearer. She swallowed back a cry of sheer misery. Angelynne was so gorgeous, and the warmth in Drake's smile as he looked at her made Nicole want to either sob with pain or knock the beauty to the ground. Maybe both.

"Why don't you offer her a contract, Griffin?" she hissed, a vicious jealousy tearing through her. She was immediately ashamed of her ignoble sentiments. It wasn't Angelynne Flynn's fault that she was beautiful and that Drake so clearly liked her. Nor was she to blame for Drake's shattering aversion to Nicole.

"Angelynne in porn? Never!" Griffin replied. His eyes were as compulsively glued to the approaching pair as Nicole's were. "So she's your replacement?" he gritted. "It must be damn hard to watch, especially with the baby and all."

"I don't need your sympathy, Griffin," Nicole snapped, fighting back tears. "All I want from you is a ride to Newark in a van big enough to carry my family and me and all our stuff."

"You've got it, doll. I don't want to stick around

here and watch Drake Austin play lover to Angelynne either."

When they were a few feet away from the porch steps, Drake and Angelynne looked up to see the duo standing on the porch. Simultaneously, their smiles faded and their laughter came to an abrupt end. Drake grimly mounted the steps two at a time until he was standing before Nicole and Thad Griffin.

For a long, tense moment there was silence as the four stared at each other. Nicole was the first to break it. "Thad is taking me to Newark just as soon as he rents the van. We should be out of here within the hour."

Griffin nodded, smiling tightly.

Drake stared from Nicole to Griffin. "You think you're going to Newark? With Thad Griffin?" His blue eyes, wide with incredulity, turned hard with anger. "Oh no, Nicole. you're not going anywhere." He turned to Griffin, his jaw clenched. "And *you're* sure as hell not taking her anywhere!"

Nicole and Griffin exchanged bewildered glances. "I—er—was just trying to be—uh—helpful, Drake," Griffin stammered.

"If you want to be helpful then you can take Angelynne to the hospital to have her ankle X-rayed," growled Drake, dumping Angelynne into a startled Thad's arms. "She twisted it while we were shooting and it's starting to swell." He turned to Nicole. "That's why I was carrying her. We've had this shoot planned for weeks, but I actually forgot about it until everyone arrived this morning."

"I'm not going anywhere with *you!*" bellowed Angelynne, wriggling furiously in Griffin's arms. He tightened his hold and glowered at her. She glared right back. "Put me down, you—you loathesome fiend!"

"He is loathesome," Nicole agreed, "but I don't believe he's genuinely fiendish." She didn't want Griffin to put Angelynne down; then Drake might pick her up again. "I'm sure it's safe to go to the hospital with him, although if he offers you the lead in his latest '*art film*,' turn him down flat." Ever the big sister, she felt obliged to include that word of warning.

"Take the rest of the crew with you," Drake said to Griffin indicating the small group standing beside the car and Jeep, "and then drive Angelynne back to New York." He reached over to give Angelynne's arm a friendly pat. "I think I got enough good shots today to come up with a winner, Angel. Now take care of that ankle and I'll be in touch when we get back to the city."

Griffin started down the steps and Angelynne yelped with fury and started pounding him with her fists and kicking her legs in scissors-like motion. "Let me go! Put me down! I hate you, Thad Griffin! I'll walk to the hospital before I let you take me. I'll walk back to New York rather than go with you."

"I don't want to take you any more than you want to go with me," retorted Griffin. "I'm doing it strictly as a favor for my *good friends*, Nicole and Drake Austin." He turned his head and gave Nicole a broad wink, then resumed quarreling with Angelynne.

"Those two seem to have taken an instant dislike to each other," Drake observed. "Or do they already know and loathe each other?"

The shouting and fighting continued until Angelynne was plunked into a gray Mercedes and Griffin climbed behind the wheel and drove away, followed by the other car and the Jeep. The silence that followed was almost stunning in contrast. Little Robbie suddenly made a loud yelling noise, remarkably similar in tone to Angelynne and Griffin's battling voices.

"He's imitating them," Drake remarked, lifting the baby from Nicole's arms. "It's scary, how quickly little kids pick things up. We'll have to be careful not to fight in front of him."

Nicole turned her head, not trusting herself to look at him. "Do you plan to continue to see Robbie?" she asked carefully, her voice quavering.

"As he'll be living with me, I'm sure to see him every day."

"No!" Nicole cried, making a frantic grab for the baby. "I won't let you take him away, I—"

Drake whirled away, keeping Robbie firmly in one arm while grasping Nicole around her waist with the other. "Who said anything about taking him away? You'll be with him, Nicole. And with me," he added, his voice deepening. "Marry me, Nicole."

She was too stunned to speak. For one full minute she stood in shocked silence, staring blindly into space.

"And what was all that crap about going to Newark with Thad Griffin, of all people?" Drake demanded while she remained mute. "Did you dream that up in a jealous fit when you saw me with Angelynne? I happen to like the girl. She's hard-working and professional and fun to be with, but I have absolutely no designs on her, I assure you. And what was Griffin doing here in the first place?"

"I thought you hated me," Nicole whispered. She still wasn't sure if she'd heard him ask her to marry him or if it was pure wish fulfillment.

He stared at her. "After last night, how could you think such a thing? I thought I made it embarrassingly obvious how wild I am about you."

She heard the uneasy edge in his voice. "You might want me in bed, but you loathe me as—as much as Angelynne loathes Thad Griffin," she said sadly.

"And that's why you decided you had to go back to Newark? Because you think I don't love you and I only want you around for sex?"

"You left me last night." She started to cry and hated herself for it. She wanted to be strong, but she hurt too much to put up a brave, stoic front. "The moment we finished making love you left me. You couldn't get away from me fast enough. You took off like a rocket shedding its last booster."

Drake looked troubled. "I know. I had a lot to think about." He slid his hand along her shoulder and followed the curve of her neck to lightly cup the curve of her jaw, tilting her head up to meet his gaze. His pale blue eyes were blazing with intensity. "I was overwhelmed by what happened between us last night, Nicole. And by the knowledge that you'd never been with Andrew. I felt as if the world had turned inside out or something. I *had* to be alone to think things through. It's how I've always coped—to go off by myself for a while and try to understand what's happening."

"I do the opposite. I try to cope while in the middle of a three-ring circus. In my life, there's never any place to go to be alone."

"So naturally you thought I'd dumped you when I walked off last night," he said thoughtfully. He stared at the tears on her cheeks and the dark circles under her eyes and his face clouded with regret. "I didn't mean to hurt you, Nicole. If I thought of your reaction to my leaving at all, I guess I thought you'd go to sleep. After all, I thought I'd made it damn obvious that I—that I was all yours, to do with as you pleased."

"You didn't make it obvious at all." She gave a sad little sniff. "I—I still can't believe that you love me and want to marry me. You don't act like a man who's in love. You seem edgy and stiff and—"

"If I appear that way, it's because what I feel for you is so powerful that it scares me." He looked at the ground, obviously embarrassed at the admission. "I was the epitome of cool and laid-back, remember? 'Stay detached, keep mellow, don't let anything or anyone shake you up'

—that was the credo I lived by. And then you came along and I turned into this unrecognizable, emotional *maniac*."

She laughed a little, the tears glistening like diamonds in her dark blue eyes. "Oh, Drake," she murmured, "I love you and I want us to be together, but if loving me doesn't make you happy then—"

"It makes me happy," he cut in fiercely. "You make me happier than I've ever been in my life. You bring such joy into my life, Nicole. The only dark spot was your alleged relationship with Andrew. It tore at me, but I was even beginning to get past that. And last night when I looked at you after we made love, I felt so emotional, so much in love. I've never felt such happiness, Nicole, and I had trouble handling it." He gave his head a shake. "I felt that I didn't deserve to feel that way. That I don't deserve you, Nicole."

The legacy of his depressing childhood, thought Nicole, understanding at once. The little boy on the outside looking in, watching his brothers, his father's legally acknowledged children, playing on their big, green lawn. The scars were deep and well hidden but they definitely were there.

"You deserve all the happiness life has to offer, Drake," she said firmly, putting both her arms around him and hugging him tight. "And I'm going to make sure that you have it. And from now on, there'll be no more going off alone with anything left unsaid between us." She smiled up at him, her blue eyes shining with love and humor. "We'll talk whatever is bothering us to death and then you can slip away to your darkroom for some blessed peace and quiet."

They put Robbie down for his morning nap a little earlier than usual, and with a determination and an eagerness which must have communicated itself to him, for the little boy settled in his crib with his bottle and his toys without any fuss at all.

Then Drake led Nicole into his bedroom and locked the door, pulling her tightly into his arms. "I love you, Nicole," he said huskily, fiercely. "I'm sorry I made you cry, I'm sorry you doubted my love for even a moment. But I'm going to make it up to you, darling. I'm going to spend the rest of our lives proving to you just how much you mean to me."

A small sound escaped from her throat and she leaned into him, twining her arms around his neck. Drake smiled against her lips, then increased the caressing pressure. Her mouth opened under his and she touched the tip of her tongue to his, longing for its slow, delicious penetration. Instead of acceding to her wishes, he continued to tease her with those brief staccato kisses, until she groaned with frustration.

"Drake, please!" she breathed, threading her fingers through his hair to grip him more firmly.

"Oh yes, baby," he murmured huskily, his blue eyes sparkling with teasing sensuality. "I know exactly how to please you." He slipped his thumb into her mouth and traced the full, soft line of her lower lip.

She closed her eyes, feeling the effects of his touch deep inside her, in the innermost feminine core of her. And then they were kissing hungrily, her lips parting for him as he penetrated her mouth with his tongue to take possession of the sweet warmth within. She clung to him, responding to him with all the love and aching ardor she felt for him.

"You never did give me an answer to my question," he said, his voice hoarse with emotion and desire as he laid her down onto the bed. "About marrying me."

She smiled at him, her eyes glowing with tenderness. "I didn't hear it as a question, I believe it was more of an imperative sentence. 'Marry me, Nicole,' you said."

He gave her a playful spank. "Quit stalling and say yes."

"Yes, Drake." She sighed happily. "Yes, yes, yes!"

They kissed deeply, intimately. "My love." His eyes held hers as he entered her with slow, smooth masculine power. The passion between them flared to white-hot intensity, carrying them higher and higher until the building pleasure exploded in a simultaneous burst of rapture, binding them together in a sexual bond as strong and endurable as the emotional bonds already forged between them.

Slowly, dreamily, they floated back to earth. When Drake opened his eyes, he met Nicole's warm limpid gaze. Their bodies were still joined; one of her legs was still curved around his. She was idly trailing her fingertips over his shoulders, gently caressing him.

She smiled at him and he smiled back. Her mouth was soft and swollen from his kisses and her eyes were shining. He thought he had never seen her look prettier. A wave of tenderness surged through him. There was no thought of leaving her now. The love and joy coursing through him were just as intense and powerful as last night, but he felt no need to go off by himself to cope with it. He just wanted to hold onto her and enjoy the precious moment.

"I didn't tell you this last night, Nicole, but taking you from virgin to lover, watching and experiencing the transition, had to be one of the most profound events in my life."

"It was for me, too, Drake," she said softly, gently feathering his mouth with her lips.

"I'd like to stay like this forever," he said huskily. He felt so totally replete that the thought of moving drained him. "But I'm afraid I'm crushing you."

"Mmm, sort of." Nicole sighed. "But I don't mind." A sweet languor flowed through her entire body. "There's something I'm curious about though," she added drowsily.

Drake stretched slowly, flexing his muscles as he reluctantly began to ease himself from her enveloping warmth. "And what's that?" he asked, his blue eyes warm and indulgent.

"Last night, when I was locked in the bathroom . . . would you really have kicked in the bathroom door?"

Drake chuckled. "I just might have. In case you hadn't noticed, I was totally out of my head at that point."

Nicole grinned in memory. "I sort of did notice that."

He settled her alongside him, and she snuggled into the curve of his body. "I did a lot of thinking last night, Nicole. And not just about us, but about your—our—family, too."

Nicole gazed at him with serious blue eyes. "I'm not exactly a free agent, Drake. Robbie, Peter, Hailey and the children—and Cheryl to some extent—depend on me."

"Marrying you is a package deal," he agreed. "And I admire your sense of responsibility, Nicole. Once I got over the initial shock of learning that you hadn't given birth to Robbie, I understood why you felt you couldn't tell me the truth. You were protecting him—he's just a baby, he needs his mother to place his interests above her own. That's the kind of love and loyalty and strength I want the mother of my children to have." He kissed her lingeringly. "Will you have my baby, Nicole?"

"Oh yes, Drake. I want a big family. I like lots and lots of children around! I'm even willing to take Andrew's two other little ones if—"

"Whoa!" Drake blanched, then laughed. "Whew!

There are no halfway measures with you, are there? But I'm glad you mentioned those other two babies Andrew left behind. I'm going to do what you suggested—what I know is the right thing to do—and inform Preston Austin that I'm assembling a team of expert lawyers specializing in family law to challenge him on behalf of Andrew's daughters' interests. If he decides to make a fair settlement with the mothers out of court, that's fine. But if not, we'll fight him all the way."

"And he'll lose," added Nicole.

"I've decided to tell my half brothers Dane and Ian about the children and why I'm going to fight Preston."

She nodded. "I hope they'll agree with us, Drake. I'd like to see the Austin brothers be friends instead of competitors."

Drake shrugged. "It could happen some day. And now we come to Peter. I'm phoning Glenview Acres today, Nicole, and I'll pull whatever strings have to be pulled to get Peter a place there. He needs to do more with his life, honey. He needs much more than we can give him by keeping him with us."

"I know. It breaks my heart to watch him merely existing when I want him to be *living* his life! Oh, Drake, Glenview Acres will be perfect for him. And he can come home for visits and we can visit him there. . . ."

"Of course. And Demon goes with him, remember?" Drake grinned. "If you want another dog around, let's get one that weighs under a hundred pounds."

"A cocker spaniel," Nicole said promptly. "And I'd like a couple of cats, too." She grew serious once more. "Drake, what about Hailey? She's so insecure. And her rotten ex-husband doesn't even pay a cent of child support."

"I know." Drake grimaced. "You and I share the same beliefs about fathers supporting their children. We'll have the guy tracked down and nailed for child support, Nicole."

"She needs to gain some confidence and independence, too," Nicole said. "Do you have any ideas on how to make Hailey less insecure and dependent on me?"

"It just so happens that I do. How about sending the Ruggerios on their way and hiring Hailey as overseer here? We'll hire a maid and a yard service, but she'll be officially in charge of the place. Do you think she can handle it? We'll visit often, of course, more in the summer than winter, but she and her kids will live here year-round."

"It would be a big step for her," Nicole said thoughtfully. "She's never lived alone. She went from our house, where I was mostly in charge, to her horrible husband, who ruled with an iron hand during their marriage."

"She won't be alone. She'll have her children and we'll be a phone call away most of the time. The rest of the time we'll be here, with her."

"What about the Ruggerios?"

Drake laughed. "What about the Ruggerios? I think I've subsidized them long enough. I'm not cut out to be one of those old-time art patrons who supports the budding talents of artistic geniuses for years. It's about time they moved on."

"They may agree with you there." Nicole's eyes danced. "Rich wasn't very happy that you had the nerve to ask Linda to make coffee this morning."

"They suggested that I wake up you or Hailey to do it!" Drake said indignantly. "They've always gotten on my nerves with their policy of doing as little as possible around here, but this morning . . ."

"They got on your last nerve?" suggested Nicole and they both laughed.

"Let's apply for the marriage license today," Drake said eagerly, gazing down at her with ardent, eager eyes. "I want to marry you as soon as possible, Nicole. I can't wait to begin our life together."

"Neither can I." She slipped her arms around his neck and nuzzled him. "I love you so much, Drake," she whispered, passionately intense. Suddenly, she was desperate to feel his lips upon hers again.

"Kiss me, Drake," she whispered and Drake was delighted to comply. Again and again, his mouth took hers, demanding and receiving her impassioned response.

"I love you, Nicole," he whispered. "I think I've been waiting my whole life for you."

Tears of joy glimmered in her eyes. "I feel the same way about you, Drake."

His hands caressed her, sensuously, arousingly, and since their lovemaking had given her such sublime completion the last time, her response to his touch was volcanic. She *needed* to be part of him in the most elemental way.

And a short, passionate while later, amidst kisses and caresses and whispered words of love, she was.

THE EDITOR'S CORNER

This coming month brings to mind lions and lambs—not only in terms of the weather, but also in terms of our six delightful LOVESWEPTs. You'll find fierce and feisty, tame and gentle characters in our books next month who add up to a rich and exciting array of folks whose stories of falling in love are enthralling.

First, hold on to your hat as a really hot wind blows through chilly London town in Fayrene Preston's marvelous *The Pearls of Sharah II: RAINE'S STORY*, LOVESWEPT #318. When Raine Bennett realized someone was following her through foggy Hyde Park one night, she ran . . . straight into the arms of Michael Carr. He was a stranger who radiated danger and mystery—yet he was a man Raine instinctively knew she could trust. Michael was utterly captivated by her, but the magnificent strand of perfect pearls draped across her exquisite body complicated things. What was she doing with the legendary Pearls of Sharah, which had just been reported stolen to his branch of Interpol? What were her secrets and would she threaten his integrity . . . as well as his heart? This is a dazzling love story you just can't let yourself miss! (Do remember that the Doubleday hardcover edition is available at the same time the paperback is in the stores. Don't miss this chance to collect all three Pearls of Sharah romances in these beautifully bound editions at only $12.95.)

Jan Hudson's **THE RIGHT MOVES**, LOVESWEPT #319, will set your senses ablaze. Jan created two unique characters in her heroine and hero; they were yin and yang, fire and ice, and they could not stay away from each other no matter how hard they tried. Chris Ponder was a spitfire, a dynamo with a temper . . . and with a tow truck. When she took one look at Nick Russo's bedroom eyes, her insides turned to tapioca, and she suddenly wanted to flirt with the danger he represented. But good sense started to prevail. After all, she hardly needed to fall for a handsome charmer who might be all flash and no substance. Still Nick teased, and she felt she might go up in flames . . . especially on one moonlit night that filled her with wonder. This is a breathlessly exciting romance!

In LOVESWEPT #320, **THE SILVER BULLET AFFAIR**, Sandra Chastain shows us once again that love sure can conquer all. When John Garmon learned that his brother Jeffrey's will instructed him to "Take care of Caitlan and the

(continued)

baby—it's mine," he immediately sought out the quicksilver lady who had charmed him at every former meeting. Caitlan proved to be like a fine perfume—good at disappearing and very elusive. She believed that John was her adversary, a villain, perhaps, who might take her baby away if he learned the truth. So how could she lose herself in the hot shivery sensations of his embrace? Bewitched by this fragile woman who broke all the rules, John grows determined to rescue Caitlan from her free-spirited life and the gang of crazy but caring friends who never leave them alone to learn to love each other. A shimmering, vivid love story that we think you'll find a real delight.

The brilliant . . . fun . . . thrilling . . . surprising conclusion to the "Hagen Strikes Again" series, by Kay Hooper, **ACES HIGH**, LOVESWEPT #321, comes your way next month. Skye Prescott was tall, dark, and dangerous, a man who'd never forgotten how Katrina Keller had betrayed him years before. In a world where survival depended on suspicion, he'd fallen in love—and it had broken him as violence never had. When the beautiful redheaded ghost from his past reappeared in his life, Skye was filled with fury, hurt, a desire for revenge—and an aching hunger to make Katrina burn for him again. Katrina had fought her memories, but once she was in his arms, she couldn't fight him or her own primal passion. She was his match, she was his mate—but belonging to him body and spirit gave him the power to destroy her. When Skye faced his most violent enemy, Trina knew she faced the most desperate gamble of her life. Now, friends, need I tease you with the fact that Hagen also gets his in this fabulous book? I know you've been wondering (as all of us here have) what Kay was going to do for that paunchy devil in terms of a love story. Well, next month you will know. And I can guarantee that Kay has been as delightfully inventive as we had hoped and dreamed she would be.

Please give a great, warm welcome to talented new author Marcia Evanick by getting and enjoying her powerfully emotional romance, **PERFECT MORNING**, LOVESWEPT #322. How this story will touch your heart! When Jason Nesbit entered Riki McCormick's front yard in search of his young daughter, he never expected to find an emerald-eyed vixen as her foster mother. He had just learned that he had a child when his ex-wife died in an accident. Traumatized after her mother's death, the girl had not spoken since. Jason marveled at Riki's houseful of love—and was capti-

(continued)

vated by the sweet, spirited woman who'd made room in her life for so many special children. Under Jason's steamy scrutiny, Riki felt a wave of longing to be kissed breathless and held tight. When his Texas drawl warned her that her waiting days were over, she unpacked her slinkiest lingerie and dreamed of satin sheets and firelight. But courting Riki with seven children around seemed downright impossible. You'll laugh and cry with Jason and Riki as they try to make everyone happy. A keeper!

Halsey Morgan is alive—and Stevie Lee wanted him dead. What a way to open a romance! Glenna McReynolds has created two wonderful, thrilling characters in LOVESWEPT #323, **STEVIE LEE.** Halsey Morgan was Stevie Lee's long-lost neighbor. She had plotted for the last few years to buy his cabin for his back taxes, sell it for a huge profit, and get out of her small town so she could see the world. Handsome Halsey had blazed a trail of adventure from the Himalayas to the Amazon—and was thought to be dead. Now he was back—ruining her plans to escape and melting her with sizzling kisses that almost made her forget why she'd ever wanted to go away. His wildness excited her senses to riot, while his husky voice made her tremble with want. Hal had never stayed anywhere long enough to fall in love, but Stevie was the answer to a loneliness he'd never dared admit. He made her take chances, climb mountains, and taught her how to love him. But could Hal persuade her to risk loving him and follow her dreams while held tight in his arms? Don't miss this great story . . . which, we think you'll agree, knocks your socks off!

Enjoy those blustery days next month curled up with six LOVESWEPTs that are as hot as they are happily-ever-after.

Carolyn Nichols

Carolyn Nichols
Editor
LOVESWEPT
Bantam Books
666 Fifth Avenue
New York, NY 10103

Special Offer
Buy a Bantam Book
for only 50¢.

Now you can have Bantam's catalog filled with hundreds of titles plus take advantage of our unique and exciting bonus book offer. A special offer which gives you the opportunity to purchase a Bantam book for only 50¢. Here's how!

By ordering any five books at the regular price per order, you can also choose any other single book listed (up to a $5.95 value) for just 50¢. Some restrictions do apply, but for further details why not send for Bantam's catalog of titles today!

Just send us your name and address and we will send you a catalog!